To Heather

To Jo

To the delightful chaps at the Sheffield Science Fiction
and Fantasy Writers Group

Ευχαριστώ

Shall we their fond pageants see?
Oh, what fools these mortals be.
- William Shakespeare, A Midsummer Night's Dream

Kallisti
A Discordian Tale

Edwin Black

This edition first published in 2020 by Edwin Black
Copyright © Edwin Black 2020
Artwork © Edwin Black 2020
Title Font: "Kramer" from 1001freefonts.com
The moral right of Edwin Black to be identified as the author of this work has been asserted by him in accordance with the Copyright, Designs, and Patents Act 1988
All rights reserved. No part of this publication may be reproduced, printed, stored or transmitted in any form without written permission of the author with the exception of reviews, criticism, and scholarly articles
Printed by KDP
ISBN: *9781653748815*

Prologue

The traveller was of a type that was seldom seen in this part of the world. Indeed, this individual was usually more likely to be seen in one of the colonies of the vast empire his country had claimed. India, China, Africa perhaps – but this part of Europe was, generally, well outside the remit of his business. The country of Greece, newly a kingdom, was one that a Britisher such as himself had only seen in letters. The philosophy, ancient politics, and literature of the place had rendered it a nation that was far away and long ago. Athens and Sparta still fought for supremacy, Draco still ruled with an iron fist, and the Colossus still stood resplendent, burning torch hand, defending the island of Rhodes. He could just about believe that he was currently climbing up one of the peaks of Olympus with a pack dangling from his shoulder.

The climb had begun in the late morning. Now the sun had been doing its work on him, drenching his shirt and reddening all his exposed skin. *I just need to get to that ledge. Then I could relieve some of the weight from my back – who would have thought that water would be so heavy?* The ascent was arduous. Loose pebbles demonstrated how to make one's way down the peak in a much quicker manner than he had clambered up. Every now and again his foot would slip, sending intense shocks through his spine. Finally, he reached the ledge. Immediately behind was a crevice running across the floor. *Best stay away from that one. Who knows how deep that goes?* Above, the summit beckoned not another hour away. At this altitude the hot stillness of the air had given away to a slight, cool breeze which brushed the traveller's dirty cheek and ruffled his greasy hair. It lessened the grip of fire that had seized him from midday onwards, bringing some much needed relief.

He gasped. The gods had chosen this place for their palaces for a reason. His eyes traced over the grey of the rock till it disappeared into the forests that skirted down to the mountain's feet. Peering at the horizon he could just about make out the taller buildings of Volos *If I were on the other side I bet I could see Thelassoniki.* From there he heard the bird song he was deep in nature. It truly was the navel of Greece. He slung his pack down to the ground. Taking a bundle of papers and a pencil, he carried on his notes from where he left up in a coffee shop in Thelassoniki. Though the pencil took a shorter time than he to climb the mountain it tended to linger on the finer details and thoughts spun out into whole paragraphs and spilled themselves into the scenery. It finally caught up with him after five pages. He put his pencil back in his pack. The end of that specific chapter waited at the summit. *Well, the heat has died down. Might be worth looking about.* He took stock any footholds he could use. At first the rock seemed to be sheer, smoothed by aeons of weather but, taking a closer look, it seemed that it would not be such a hard climb after all. Rope, of course, would have to be used but, other than that, all would be well.

He stepped back and found himself falling backwards. The ground opened up as the mountain swallowed this tiny morsel. *What...oh...* He saw the sunlight disappear from the crack. There was no thought as his brain quickly made the calculations and had accepted the doom that was to come in a few mere seconds. There was simply no point in fear. He could not run, after all. After these last seconds he would surely be smashed on the cavern floor, a stain against ancient stone. The ground struck. All his weight came back to him, bouncing on his bones, pushing down on his chest and limbs, threatening to snap his ribs. He had expected pain, more of a crunch at least, but that was absent. The very fact that he was still breathing was a surprise. Neither did it feel as though he landed on the rock. Rock does not tend to feel soft or break a fall in such a tidy fashion.

What on Earth has just happened? For a couple of minutes, he could only lay upon the spongy ground, trying to orient himself. The mouth that had swallowed him had become a thin slit through which the late afternoon made every attempt to fall. As for the cave, it was utterly devoid of any man-made features. Indeed, the place had been otherwise untouched if the amounts of dirt and old detritus were anything to gage it by. As his eyes wandered, his senses, one by one, slowly returned. Smell introduced him to his saviour. He wanted to stand, to quickly get off this thing, but he was equally aware that he should not try to stand straight away for fear of having damaged something. *If I break a leg here there will be no rescue.* He carefully rolled off the soft mass, disturbing the small ants that had begun to walk over his body in search of the promised sweetness that surely was within their jaws. After rubbing at his legs and ribs he concluded that no structural damage had been done and stood, looking at the form of his saviour. *Ah. I thought as much.*

He looked upon the dead face of an unfortunate sheep. From what he could ascertain the poor thing had been dead for a couple of days at most. The lack of blood around the body and the rising smell were both indicative of that, as well as the flies that wafted around the torso. *At least her eyes are closed.* The traveller took stock. The pack lay a couple of feet away, a wet shadow growing beneath. *God damn. Still, the notes are in pencil. A bit smudged but not the end of the world.* Directly behind opened a dark cave. *Could it be a tunnel? If so it might help in escaping.* What was clear was that climbing out was not an option. The walls bulged outward – by the time they got to the ceiling it would have been impossible to reach the gap. *Not nearly enough rope.* He took his pack and removed the broken canteen. *No saving this.* He threw it aside. *That will make life a little more difficult. I will definitely need something by the time I get to the next taverna. Hopefully there will be a stream or pool before then.*

As he took the first step to the cave he felt a twinge knot in his back. *Ah. Something has been jarred. That will be felt tomorrow.* Now, a little carefully, he entered the cave. After mere moments, he had been enveloped in shadow, heavy and very old. Silence was all around. No breeze passed through. He raised his hands to his mouth.

"Hi!"

There was no reply apart from his echo and, from far away, some frightened bird. *A bird! Well, it is certainly a tunnel – not a long one at any rate.*

"Hi!"

This time his echo was alone. *Of course. Whoever owned that sheep probably does not even know it has gone missing yet. Not a friendly yiassas or hairete for miles from here.* The darkness was so absolute that no shape made itself known to break the solid black. However much he adjusted his eyes he still found himself shuffling forward, hoping that no rocks would send him tumbling down. *To fall now would be my doom. Even if a shepherd did come looking for a missing sheep he would never find me in this place. As for banging my head, well, I have been rather lucky thus far.* He shuddered. So far the only thing keeping him alive was luck, something that, in his ample experience, was a finite resource.

The silence was ancient, a composite of long dead drums banging ecstatically and the ritual chanting that accompanied it. Those drums were still booming as Homer spoke of Troy with blind eyes and mighty voice. They played as Plato crawled out of his cave and found his enlightenment. Even as Icarus fell from the sky they boomed deep in the palaces of Olympus. The traveller could feel its age. It was the same feeling he had when he first encountered Stonehenge or when he looked upon the great Pyramids of Egypt and the Ottoman minarets. Only, this silence held so much more weight. It would be there for longer than a hundred of his lives and would linger for long after Olympus itself was scattered to the winds. In his profession, he had grown accustomed to grandness in ruin but here that had intensified to its breaking point. *Ought I drag the sheep with me as an offering? Shall I dance to the dead drums? Have I become Euripides come to the Thesmophoria?*

Dizziness struck. *I should not be here. But I have crossed the threshold. Will there be a dweller? I cannot stop my ascent from the floor of my cave. With no return, I must keep on.* He shuffled on for a few minutes more. Finally, light appeared around a corner. The way was clear – no stalactites threatened his head, no hidden rocks crept toward his ankles. He could walk forward, discarding the absurd shuffle he had adopted. *Freedom! I will be away from this mountain by the dusk, I should think. At a village or inn by the night. Excellent.* Yet this elation was marked. There was something fearful about the light. He could but sneak up to it, as though it would try to run away if it were startled. When he reached the mouth of the tunnel he pushed out his hand to touch the warmth. *At this altitude? Coolness at this time, surely?* His ears rang with the drumming silence, forcing him to make the final step.

He gasped as he looked about him. The stage onto which he stepped was a large bowl that flattened out on the far end. Ruins, tall and still proud, populated the area. It was a beautiful desolation created of open verandas, shattered pillars, and half-covered mosaics trying to reach through the dirt of many years. The stone was a mixture of time stained marble and yellow sandstone, contrasting with the grey of Olympus. The little wood that had been used in the construction was long blackened. And the silence still hung in the air, thudding in rhythm with the traveller's heart. He all but fainted at the sight. Looking down he saw that he was standing on the torso of a fallen statue – the bow still clutched tightly in her hand, the helm smashed against the floor. There were more of these effigies around the place, all staring upon him with powerful, terrible eyes. *This…this is Olympus. They lived here once.* Power still lingered there, echoing in the drum beat. The gods were merely absent, not dead as some might have guessed. If they were to return they would find their fortresses taken by the forces of time and they would rebuild with the greatest Spartan fury.

That drumming was strongest in the centre of the desolation. There was a grand stone table still covered in their plates and cups. His heart leapt, temptation following it closely. He would not take anything from the table – such an action would be utterly foolish. Who knew what trouble he would cause in doing such a thing? Such thoughts died when he saw it. On a raised pillar in the middle of the table it shone in the afternoon light. Thousands of years it had sat in its place at table, untouched by time and nature. He could even read the inscription carved into it, written in inlayed jet. *Kallisti*. It was just about the right size to fit in one's hand. And it was just about the right weight to not be a bother to someone who would spend the rest of the day climbing and hiking.

The thief stole away.

And here our story begins with a click of the fingers.

Chapter One

The woman walked down the dusty road. It led down from the slopes Olympus, losing itself in the skirts of the forest. Like those trees the woman was quite tall and slender, and was topped with long, thick black hair which was halfway hidden under a wide brimmed hat. As she walked her red skirts drifted in the breeze just above her booted ankle. The sun illuminated her white blouse, and her stuffed haver-sack bounced with every step as though it were making to escape, planning to go on its own journey. *Well. It was a tough climb but I suppose it was worth it. Better than falling.* She came to a sign post, taking the opportunity to give her arms a tired stretch. Before she could read it there suddenly came a buzz just on the edge of hearing. *Oh great. It's began already.* She shook her head violently, making the sound subside. *There. Bought some time. Now, whereabouts am I?*

Thelassoniki, 55 M

Larissa, 54 M

Álsostoukyparísi, 2 M

I knew there was a cypress grove nearby! They seem to have built over it, though. Still, it might be worth stopping off there. Certainly better than sleeping in a ditch somewhere. Having made her decision, she adjusted her bag strap and carried on into the afternoon. She wore a mask of calm which told all that this was little more than any other stroll, that she was another traveller making her way through the landscape. However, if we were to look closer we would see faint cracks and blemishes. The base material was that of great hurry mixed, perhaps, with some pain. These cracks could widen at any given notice. For now, the woman was simply approaching the farming village of Álsostoukyparísi but who knows what will happen later? One's resolve, no matter who they are, can only last for so long.

The village sat upon a small hill, looking as though it had been spilled there from a high table. The houses, though uniform in colours of white, blue, and orange, were of every type from clustered maisonettes to detached huts. All in all, it was a ragged architectural gang. *Poor little place.* It was vaguely built as a circle in the centre of which, where once a sacred stone table stood, was a picturesque fountain. Sat on its ledge were a couple of old salts. *Peasants living from the land, methinks. The type of place where travellers tend to pass through and from which its denizens never leave. Still, might yet be interesting. Little places hold big secrets.* She finished her survey of the village, sitting at the fountain with the old men. One was thin, wearing a fez and the other was quite large. He would have been described as "burly" in younger days, and smoked from a long-necked pipe.

"*Kallispira*", she greeted.

The men nodded in reply.

"Is there anywhere I can stay for the night? I'm not from around here, you see, and don't particularly want to sleep on the road."

The larger man turned his head sleepily. "Ana could probably help you. She runs an open house. I don't know whether she's got a lodger at the minute, though."

The smaller man piped up. "Ah, that one left this morning – saw them myself. She'll have room. Hell, even if she didn't she'd make it."

"Aye. She's a good one, is our Ana."

"Whereabouts does she live?" The woman asked.

"Oh, just off the centre here", the bigger man pointed. "You just need to go up that street there and you'll find her. It's the bigger house – the Eye is posted above the door."

"Thank you very kindly."

"No matter, young lady. We're lucky to attract any attentions nowadays."

As they chuckled to each other she bid them *andil* and followed the direction they had given her. The street was only a pedestrian walkway paved with multicoloured pebbles. The houses either side trapped the heat in their tight shadows. *Well, at least there's no outdoor gutter. And it doesn't seem all that bad.* It did not take her long at all to find the house. It was slightly larger than the others, taller by a floor and had a small yard accessible via a small group of steps. The most noticeable difference from the other houses was the *nazar* hanging above the door, quiet in its staring modesty. The woman met its gaze as though she were waiting for it to blink. Then, satisfied, stepped over the threshold. *Comfy. Everything that one would possibly need.* There was not much furniture – a couple of chairs, a cabinet, and coffee table was all. On the far wall there was an open doorway to what looked to be the kitchen and another that lead to the stairs. There was a slight tinge of peppermint that only served to emphasize the domesticity.

"*Hairete! Kyrya Ana?*" The woman called.

Suddenly, a sound of bustling came from the kitchen. Then, a voice.

"Are you looking for a room?"

It was small, sweet, and a little croaky. The woman knew what Ana would look like even before she creaked into the room. She was rotund, white haired and a good foot and a half shorter than her. A pair of large, round *pince-nez* clutched to her nose. She peered at the woman.

"I am, madam", she said with a curtsey.

"Well, you're in luck as it so happens. It's just become available today. I even managed to change the linen some half an hour ago – lavender ought to have done its job by now. Do come in. And stop standing as though you haven't an idea in your head, will you?"

As the woman sat down Ana passed her the guest book.

"Just sign that for me, would you dear? And, as you do, could you tell me how you came by here?"

"Oh, yes", the woman replied as she scratched her name, "A couple of old men told me."

Ana sighed. "Was one wearing a fez, by chance?"

"Yes."

"Oh, damn it", Ana took the guest book. "I do wish that Nikos wouldn't do that. Men…they always think that they're being oh-so-helpful."

Ana traced her finger along the page and frowned. "Is that really your name?"

The voice was not harsh, not even reproachful, though the curiosity was impossible to hide.

"Absolutely." The woman grinned.

"*Eris Discordia*", Ana read. "Now why would your parents name you something like that? Much too pretty for a name like that"

"Heh. Never really thought about it, myself"

"Goddess of Chaos, though…why on Earth name you

after *her?* Diana would've been much better."

Oh! So, she knows the old stories. And an...interesting choice all things considered. She doesn't believe, though. Might have to take this further, methinks. No point in lying.

"Well...I'm not named after her...so much as, well, am her. Yes. I am Eris Discordia, Goddess of Chaos, Bringer of Discord, *et cetera.*"

Ana gave her a quizzical look. *What's her game?* Her gaze shifted to her eyes. *No. Not a sign of deceit. Mischief though...lots of that.*

"I'm old", Ana said. "Not daft. And neither are you. I don't know if you're up to something or if you're one of those *bohemians* but I shan't stand for this kind of silliness. Though if you insist upon being called Eris I'll call you that."

"Well, what if I could prove it to you?"

"And how will you do that?"

Eris stood and, with a flourish, clicked the fingers of her right hand. "By tomorrow", she said, "something will happen. I don't know what it will be, but it will be something."

"Oh, will it now? Alright. I'll accept that if it makes you happy."

Suddenly, there came a long whistle from the kitchen. "Ah, that will be the tea. Would you like some?"

That explains the peppermint.

"Yes, please."

Ana shifted from the room. *Watch her. A bit of an odd one but harmless, thinks I. But still worth watching. Why're the young always so wild? Strange for the sake of it, so I wager. And where's she headed? Is she in trouble? Will she be safe? Christ, I'm not her mother. I oughtn't get involved.* She gathered the tea things onto a tray and returned to the living room. A breeze had joined them, making its way through the front door as though it was a welcome and wanted guest. She set the tray on the coffee table.

"Would you like to pour it?"

"I shall", Eris replied. She performed the task with ease and, Ana noticed, not without ceremony. She sat on the chair opposite and was handed a cup.

"Thank you kindly", she said as she drained it all in one. "You know – my husband used to tell me that my tea was the best in the region. He'd know, of course, he wandered it enough!"

Eris took a sip. *She might think me mad but, well, she's still friendly enough. What has she seen? There's happiness in her eyes. But something else, too. Loneliness, perhaps? That same desire which all elders feel when they see the young – that longing for days that have been long spent. Those days disappear into memory and memory into dream. They'll never come back. Memory is the mind's last grasp on youth. That's the order of things. Sister Harmonia's plan when it comes to mortals if nothing else. Though there's still…something else. It's small, but there. What is that glimmer? Is it curiosity? Of course, it is. It needs coaxing, though. Nurturing.*

"Well, I'm doing my own trek."

"I can see that! Where are you headed? Larissa, maybe? I haven't been there for years. Beautiful city if the young ones are to be believed."

"I'll be passing through Larissa and Volos – I'm

headed to Rhodes."

Ana leaned back. "Rhodes. Now, that is a long way. A whole ocean away. Why are you going all the way there? I assume you've come from Thelassoniki already."

"Something was stolen from me. From my house. I know that it is in Rhodes. The thief seems to have done all that he could to get away from me. He has taken something of great value, something I made with my own hands. If you were in the same place wouldn't you do the same?"

"Heh. If I were a younger woman I certainly would."

They sat, drank of their tea, and let the conversation walk along its strange road. Pieces of local news and whispers, a story or two of Ana and her husband, but no word of the thief. *Well, he would not show off his quarry to all and sundry.* As time went on Eris could not help but take a liking to the older woman. Though age harried her bones and dried her joints there was still a lot of life afforded to her. Ana, for all intents and purpose, was the type of woman who would live to see a century go by. Something about her manner and the constant stream of wisdom had lulled Eris into her domestic spell. She had been offered an invitation into Ana's quiet world – an invitation she accepted wholeheartedly.

"But look at us wittering!" Ana exclaimed suddenly. "The sun is going down and I haven't even shown you your room!"

She leapt up, taking Eris' hand. Her pull was surprisingly impressive, a quick yank that nearly had her flying from the chair. It was perfectly honest, if a little earnest, and filled with excitement. *She truly likes keeping her house open. There is no bad here.* Ana opened the stairs door, all but forgetting that Eris had to grab onto her haver-sack. The stairs were small and numerous, ending at a small landing with a pair of doors that faced each other.

"That one's mine." Ana pointed to the far side door. "This one will be yours."

They went through the door. Plain, small, and enough for a night or two.

The evening went on as the afternoon had – with much talk and hospitality. Ana brought out a fragrant stew from the kitchen, setting the pot down in the living room and filling bowls until it was finally empty. Only then was Eris allowed to leave for her room and made ready for the night's sleep. She settled comfortably into her bed. *To think – I had reservations about this lot. I have seen them in how they have acted toward the gods before and how angry they always seemed. Starting a war between them is an easy enough exercise, so I recall. But they seem alright. Perhaps, and it's took them a while, they have changed a bit.* Eris closed her eyes and saw the wind blowing through the cypress trees that had stood there before and heard the pipes of her old friend Pan.

Ana's last thought before dropping into Morpheus' kingdom was that if she were a younger woman she would be very tempted. Very tempted indeed.

Chapter Two

Marble columns held the ceiling of her dreams aloft. The floor was an elaborate mosaic of intersecting, infinite swirls and spirals that dared any sane mortal to look upon them without the protections only insanity could freely give. In the centre of this pattern was the effigy of Kallisti itself. The tiles were the purest gold, having long ago been transmuted by the most skilled of alchemists and settled by the maddest of architects. This was the House of Discordia. She stood on an open veranda which looked out over the entirety of Greece from the mainland of Thessaly and the Peloponnese to the myriad islands spanning the Aegean. And it was on the island of the Colossus that a small glimmer waved to her. The Apple was waiting for its creator's hand.

Suddenly a loud, sustained scream tore through the sky. It hit the house with such force that the columns were toppled, dashing the mosaic. The pillars holding up the veranda fell with them, flinging Eris into the restless sea. Her eyes wrenched open. *What's happened? What's that noise?* Panicked gibbering flooded from the room opposite. *Ana!* In one movement, she leapt from the bed and dashed to the old woman's room. She saw blood on the bed. Her eyes widened.

"Ana! Is everything –"

Well.

Ana was hyperventilating in the corner, eyes wide and watery, never leaving her small mirror. Waves of shock shook her body. What had frightened her was apparent. She had lost all her age beyond twenty years.

"I-I-I-I-I what? Who? H-H-How?"

"I did say that *something* would happen", Eris stated with a slight smirk.

"Yes. You did."

And, with that, Ana fainted.

~*~

"So, you really are Eris Discordia?"

"Yes, but you can just call me Eris."

"And you caused this?" Ana gestured over her body.

"In a manner of speaking it was you who was the trigger."

"And the Apple?"

"At Rhodes."

"Well."

"Well."

They ate breakfast quietly. *This is strange. I haven't thought this clearly for years.* Ana could not help but glance at Eris. *She really is quite attract – no. No, no. Not these thoughts. I put them to bed decades ago. I might look twenty but I'm certainly not. Besides, it's wrong. I can't. There was only one. But still. And I am younger now. Ah. This will take some getting used to. Some wearing in.*

As though she knew precisely what debate was raging in Ana's mind Eris said, "I can see why they used to call you the prettiest girl in the village."

"Oh! I, well, thank you."

Breakfast continued. *I can't live here any more. The village is just too small now. It's time to go. To Larissa, perhaps? I wonder if she would let me follow her. Yes. It's about time I did something for myself. No more open houses, no more boxy little village with daft old men who think they run my affairs. All change now.*

"Can I come with you as far as Larissa?"

Eris smiled. "Of course! Company is always welcome."

"Excellent! When do we start?"

"After breakfast. I might be a goddess but I still like food."

"Of course, yes, food."

Packing took very little time. When Eris looked at Ana's face she saw an expression that was worth an entire speech – this trip to Larissa was not a simple flying visit. *There is more to wise old Ana than first glances suggest, it seems. What is for certain is that she is not planning on coming back any time soon.* The village bubble had burst and the whole of Thessaly was waiting for her, the road to Larissa beckoned. However, as they left the house, Ana stopped for a moment.

"Careful there!" Eris called, "I knew a man who turned back once. Let's just say that it did not end well."

Ana ignored her, grabbed onto the *nazar* and yanked. The eye fell from its place without resistance. She then tied the string around her neck, allowing it to stare out from her chest. It was small but would be able to draw one's eyes if it were to be noticed. This eye was not for blinking – it could hold another's gaze for as long as it wished and that gaze would be broken only on its own terms.

"It's for good luck", Ana stated.

"I highly doubt that anything will want to attack us on the road with such a dutiful lookout."

"Less patronising, more walking."

"Yes miss!"

They sauntered down the street, coming into the village centre. The sunlight was warm, glinting off the fountain and not a sign of the old men was present. *A pity – I fancy that Nikos would have a heart attack seeing me like this!* A large group of men and women with hoes and shovels slung over their shoulders appeared, pouring from the houses and up from the outlying street. They were akin to a ragtag militia of farmhands, all headed for the fields. Even at this early hour the taverna had its doors open, the smell of cooking bacon creeping along the ground. Ana looked from house to house, the cracks upon their faces all too familiar. *Goodbye Álsostoukyparísi. You've been the barrow of my life but, now reborn, I leave your clutches. Larissa beckons – she calls to me. Our union is finished, finally finished.*

The crowd began to thin out when they reached the outskirts, dissolving into the plains beyond. Their voices and boot-falls disappeared over rises and under drops as the day's work beckoned them from miles away. For now, the village would fall silent from their bawdy songs and heated grumblings but would surely reawaken with the setting of the sun – then would beer be drank, stories be told, and life, as it so often does, would continue on. Soon enough our pair were left to their own journey. The air was clear, if a little dusty and dry, the sky completely clear and blue. Heat moved like a cat, curling itself around their legs and bodies, begging for any attention they would be willing to give. Eris took a deep breath.

"There's not another place between here and Larissa", Ana said. "We might have to sleep rough. Though, if we get a move on, we could get to a decent spot. I hope you've got blankets in that haversack of yours."

"Of course I do. I am more worried about you – you spent no time at all packing."

"I've got what I need. Food, water, money, and blankets."

"Oh good – I was worried that we might have had to share."

With that, they set off proper into the morning. The road was an aggrandised dirt track, rutted and cracked. Here and there rocks stuck up from the ground, threatening to scrape at their ankles. How a cart was to use this road was well beyond Eris, but from the tracks that were present she supposed that they must somehow manage. *Ana could probably tell me. I wonder why it is that she is being so quiet.* The landscape embraced them, taking them completely into itself – they were but two figures that disappeared into the hazy oil painting of Greece. She could see the old shrines and inhaled deeply, trying to find the ghost of incense or of the burnt offering roasting in the auger. Yet nature, that great demolisher, had swallowed them completely. The shrines had sunk into the ground and became nothing but pebbles on the long road to Larissa. She gave one of them a sharp kick. *Greedy nature. Pan would be proud, though. All he had to do was watch. Nature looks after itself for the most part, even if these strange mortals make war against it.* She sighed and looked to Ana. *Got to break the monotony or else I'll just get morose.*

"So – who are you, exactly?" She asked.

"Pardon?"

"Well, you know who I am. I've not hidden anything – completely open. Do not get me wrong, you seem lovely, but I have no idea just who Ana is and I detect that you are hiding something. You don't have to say a thing, of course, but it is just us and the road at this point."

Ana's pace slowed. *What do I tell her? Everything, I suppose. Why is she asking me?*

"I'm just curious is all", Eris answered.

Wait. Did she just –

"No. I can guess them, though."

"Do you do this often?"

"Not especially. I am just wondering what your angle is."

Well. There's no harm in it. Might put my mind to rest, at least.

"What do you want to know?"

"Oh, just the story of now-young Ana."

Ana smiled. "I think I know where to start."

"Please – do!"

"It's something that I have been carrying for much too long. I've not even told the priest at Confession". She sighed. *This is it. No judgement here now.* "My first love wasn't my husband."

"Oh, how scandalous!"

"It wasn't like that. My husband was a good man, but we could never connect properly. Not like the lover I had before. No. I met her when I was eighteen", she wavered, fighting herself even now to keep it in. Eris gave her a side glance, the left side of her mouth rising slightly in a lopsided smirk. *That explains the looks.*

"Please, continue. I promise not to tease you so much. You're fine to be as free as you like – you need not hide a thing."

"Fine. I used to work with my father on his stall in the

market. My mother was a seamstress, you see, and he would sell whatever she made along with the other stock. She could make such beautiful things. But anyway, it was on that stall where I first met Eudora. Love, as I have experienced it, makes all others disappear. When the one you desire comes into view it is as though a light is sent from Heaven. It illuminates them completely, showering them in soft light. Their steps are holy, their voice is a hymn", she giggled, "The slightest thing they say sends you a-flutter. This was the first time I ever felt that way toward anyone. I can't explain it that well."

"No – you are doing well. Besides, we have all been there at one time or another."

"Indeed, we have. It seemed to me that she would visit the stall often, more often than others at any rate. I couldn't help it – I fell for her from the first moment. I genuinely thought that she had to return that affection. But how could she? How could she have known? It took a couple of months but I finally grew a spine. I wrote a note and hid it in her basket."

"Risky. I like it!"

"Heh – thank you kindly. At the time I shook with all the fear of a leaf in Autumn. I was in love with another woman – if that came out then the both of us would be punished. But youth gives you fear and courage equally. For every nightmare of hate I was blessed with a dream of love. We weren't doing anything wrong. At that point we weren't doing anything at all! People are stupid things, really."

"I wouldn't say so much 'stupid' as 'limited'."

"How very polite. Anyway, we lived on the outskirts of Larissa and close by to the house was a hill. It was completely secluded – once darkness fell not a soul could make out person from tree. We were to meet there for that reason. Yet, for the days before the meeting she…stopped visiting the stall. On the night itself the fear pounced. I had to fight it off – and that I did. I crept from my parent's house and ran for the hill. And there I waited. It was midnight and she had not arrived. The fear won. I was about to leave when, coming over the crest of the hill, was Eudora. And you know what she said to me?"

"What?" Eris whispered.

Ana laughed. "*Well, I got your note kyrya Ana so I thought I should bring some food along.* That was our first stepping out."

"Haha, how romantic. Though, I've a feeling that a 'but' is on the way."

"Yes, yes, there's always a 'but' in these things, isn't there? We weren't caught or anything – she had to leave with her family for Cyprus a couple of years later. Her father was a Cypriot, you see, and he finally got the money to go back. Before they left she gave me this", she gestured to the Eye. "'*For good luck*', she told me, '*God only knows that we could both do with some*'."

"What was the thing with your marriage, though?"

"Oh, that was in the same year. Worked out for himself what I'm like but he never judged. Never even a mention. Hell, he kept his hands to himself. Truth be told, I reckon that he was happy for the friendship more than much else. I'd known him for years before and, I suppose, he got his on his travels."

Eris nodded. "Well, thank you for telling me that, friend Ana."

"That's quite alright. It's good to have it in the open". With that, she placed the large *pince-nez* back on their place on her nose.

They walked on in silence for a while. Not the awkward silence of a pair of strangers but one of contemplation, of remembrance. Peace descended upon the road to Larissa like a fine rain – even the harsh crowing from the scraggly trees seemed that little less raw. *Well, Ana, you did keep yourself well hidden, didn't you? Mortals are buckets of secrets and stories, methinks. Infinitely interesting beings, they are. There might be a limited number of stories that can exist but they have such variety that it no longer matters.* Eris turned to Ana again.

"I once knew a woman like you, you know."

"Oh yes?"

"Yes. She was a wonderful poet. I have got to say that my favourite type of person tends toward the artistic type, the reason being that you never quite know what is going on in their heads."

"Ha! Eudora once said something similar!"

"Did she? Well, Eudora was a very wise woman."

The sun shared in the camaraderie, moving across the sky in the same air of comfortable joviality as the pair on the road. Ana walked with a wholly new gait. No longer was she a woman burdened – she walked as someone freed from a long incarceration. Her eyes were those of Sisyphus when he finally reaches the top of the hill. *You can find another Eudora – there is always that possibility. If Sappho could see you she would be laughing, I should think.* The afternoon sank and the air turned orange. By the time they stopped walking their feet hummed with the ache of thirty heavy footed miles. They scouted for a place just off the road, eventually settling on a grassy verge. A stream floated slowly by a little way back, and was so clear that the detritus could be seen on the riverbed. After checking for ants Eris set about making a makeshift fire.

"There's no cover", Ana said.

"Yes, but it ought not rain tonight and the air is much too dry for dew. We should be fine. Besides", she grinned, "we have your dutiful lookout."

"Hah. Under the stars it is, then."

"Always a good thing."

Ana detached the skillet that hung from her pack and placed it over the now healthy flame. As it heated she took out some tinned meat and unceremoniously dropped it into the pan with a sizzling *plop*. As the odour wafted through the midge filled air Eris could not help but think of Diana. *She will not be impressed, that's for certain, but if she wants to hunt, kill, skin, and gut a rabbit in this heat then that is up to her. Still, I hope father enjoys fried luncheon meat – not the best offering he has ever had but not the worst.* After five minutes, during which Eris readied the blankets, the meat was ready.

"It's...better than nothing..." Ana grimaced.

"I have had worse. Trust me – I was around for the fall of Thebes. Anything to drink?"

"Just some water. I'll boil some up for coffee in the morning."

"Goodness! You really did come prepared!"

It was a calm scene. The campfire waved jollily in its shallow pit, eventually crackling a *kallinichta* to the pair as they lay to sleep. Long ago, even further back than Eris' memories, a circle of trees had stood where they now slept, and was a home to a group of dryads. Those friendly spirits, if they had not moved on so long ago, would have giggled, and blessed them both with the most pleasant of dreams. But now there was only their forgotten memory that could bewitch them. They slept happily beneath the shining light of secretive stars.

Chapter Three

Eris shifted uneasily, clawing herself back from sleep. She disentangled herself from Ana's resting embrace and looked upon her slumbering form. She smirked. *Kalimera, Ana.* She lifted herself up, stretched, and blundered over to the baggage that lay close by. *Where is that water bottle? Might be a good idea to get the coffee on before having a wash. Ah! Here it is!* She turned her head back around. *Still sleeping. Well, the smell of coffee wakes you up like nothing else.* She lit a new fire in the ruins of the old and set the pot over it. *Right, I can leave that to its business. Time for a wash.* As she walked by Ana stirred, escaping from the strange lands of dream.

The coffee met her before the sound of the pot's whistle, making her wince. *Coffee. Ground. Me. Where's...?*

"Eris?"

"Down here!" The voice called back. "Just in the stream – I've put the coffee on so help yourself!" This was followed by a low splashing. *Ah.*

"Thank you", it came out as a tired murmur.

"You're welcome!"

Ana dragged herself up and quickly searched for her *pince-nez*, shoving them on her nose. *Christ. I'm going to need a wash after this.* The coffee was bitter, the metal cup in no way helping its infusion, adding its tinny spectre to the mix. *Could be worse. Might not be here at all.* After ten minutes Eris returned, her hair damp, and sat down with the air of absolute contentment. Sighing, she took her first drink of the day.

"God", Ana said, "I'm stiff."

"Well, we did...sleep...on the ground."

"Yes…and I'll be avoiding that in future if I can help it."

"Good decision. Clearly, a sage is amongst us."

"Very funny."

"What is funnier is the idea that we will be walking into Larissa in our short-stays. Come on, get washed and changed."

They performed the daily ritual of washing and breakfasting, and quickly found themselves on the road to

Larissa. The transparent fog of early morning still found itself crawling along the ground, holding onto their ankles like a stalking cat begging. If they were to keep to this pace then they would reach the city by the early afternoon. Indeed, the day was set to be somewhat cooler than the one before, making the trek that little easier. Yet Ana seemed to slow after half an hour, folding into herself, not nearly as talkative she had been before. She fell behind and they had slowed to crawling as time passed. Eris turned to her, seeing that her head was focussed on the ground.

"What's wrong?"

"I…well…it's nothing."

"Are you sure?"

"Yes."

"Want to talk about it?"

Ana sighed. "I miss her."

Eris approached her and took her arm gently.

"My dear, I have looked at you lot from on high on occasion and what has always astounded me is the mortal ability to stay so attached to the past. Missing her is to be completely expected - Eudora was your first and only. But look at me"

Ana looked up.

"She would want you to be happy. You might think that you can't be without her but you can – there is no shame in it. Life is a chaotic road with many junctions. Sometimes we meet someone on the road and they join us for a long stretch. Only, one day, something beckons them to take the left turning where you are going rightward. Such is life. In your case you have new miles to tread, a new goal. This time I reckon that the next you meet will stay with you for the course, to the house that lies at the end."

Ana's eyes watered. "…I think I see."

"Come along, then", she passed Ana a handkerchief, "We mustn't be sleeping rough tonight as well. The knot in my back holds the key to ruling Asia."

Ana giggled. "I'm surprised that I can still move."

The dirt track they had been following finally joined the main road. It was not as rough as the track, their feet were no longer under constant threat from stones and unseen potholes. Larissa, it seemed, had unfurled its red carpet for all to use. Wheel marks crossed over its surface and as they walked they were being passed by an increasing amount of traffic. *Well, this makes sense. Larissa is the first large city since Thelassoniki – this is now the road most travelled. Progress is being made.* Eris had been fully expecting to feel some excitement, happiness at least, but all she felt was a tightness pull on her chest. Trepidation perhaps, but not fear. Not yet. *It's only a city.* She was the goddess of chaos – she could face any anything that the metropolitan insanity had to show her.

As they walked over the crest of a hill the fledgling view of the city was obscured by a dust cloud kicked up from a passing cart. Once it cleared, Eris could make out the way in which the city wound around itself, the streets weaving in and out and opening into void like plazas and piazzas. *Like the Minos labyrinth – now that was a good trip, especially after Perseus got rid of the previous occupant.* For all the friendliness it threw out, however, there was the foundation of something else, something wrong. She could not quite place it. Just looking at the place she realised that it was not a city that had gone mad but, rather, it teetered on the edge. Ana wore a wan smile. *I've not been here for so long. It's grown so much in that time.* She looked about and suddenly pointed.

"Do you see that hill there?"

It was covered in houses now, dazzling in the sun, but the lump remained, pushing them up like a lotus flower.

"Yes", Eris replied, "Is this where you tell me that it's the hill where you and Eudora went that night?"

"Got it in one."

"Strange how these things tend to work out. Nostalgia is the most powerful force in the Universe, it seems. Well, second to chaos of course."

"Ha! Your road ends where mine began!"

They followed the road, staying wary of the growing amounts of traffic. Joining them were numerous carts piled high with mysterious wares, along with other footbound travellers hoping to find their way in the world. Soon they found themselves in a cloud of pure noise amongst the donkeys, horses, and large trucks that growled their way through the tide. However, it was the human traffic that most certainly made up most of this mercantile parade. They were buried under many packs, their knees bent under the weight of entire houses balanced upon their shoulders. There were labourers looking for work in different climes, families looking to find a niche, and then those with gold already shining in their eyes. People without a *polis* – men of everyone to anyone, each a man Jack running with message in hand to Marathon. Eris and Ana were welcomed into the city just the same as the others, swallowed by the multitude.

The streets were crowded, the only place of quiet being found in Eris' mind. The thought that had been growing since the morning finally found its form. "What's your plan from here?"

"I'll find my sister. She still lives in the family home. Long since a widow – just like me."

"How will you explain all this?"

"Hmmm…Well, I haven't spoken to her in years. I'll be able to tell her that I'm Ana's daughter…Elina. I doubt that she'll question the story. From there I'll start seam-stressing again."

"Good. I was vaguely worried that you wouldn't have anywhere else to go."

"What'd you have done if that was the case?"

Ask you to join me.

"I'm not quite sure."

The pressure on Eris' chest that had began on the road had now grown to a squeeze. She could breathe freely but pain spread its tendrils, wrapping themselves toward her armpits. It was all too close, forced into a person sized space where there was only just enough room to move. If she listened closely she could just about make out a slight buzzing. It stayed beneath the rest of the noise, hiding away. No amount of head shaking would stop it – from here it would simply build. *What's going on? Kallisti? Is this your doing? I'm travelling as quickly as possible. It cannot be your doing. You can't hurt me. It'd be like Poseidon's Trident deliberately falling on his foot!*

The buildings were very different from the ones seen in the village. They were large, imposing, and even in the poorer streets they showed off what grandeur they could, like raggedy *flaneurs* on their way to the club. Deeper into the city they walked, seeing it morph and change around them. At one moment it was akin to a beehive, the next it would open up into a wide, green plaza or park. It was at once open and closed, small and large. But even when they were in these open spaces the pressure in Eris' chest remained and the faint ringing was persistent.

"What do we do now?" Ana asked.

"I need to find someone who will take me to Volos From there I can catch a ferry to Skiathos. From there, Rhodes."

"In that case the best place to go would be a taverna. I've got to say, though, Larissa has changed far more than I expected."

"How long has it been?"

"I've not been here since my mother's funeral. That'll have been…oh…1870."

"That is not long at all."

"Not to you, perhaps. Near enough a lifetime to me."

They ducked into a street that was lined with numerous food-stalls, perpetually busy. The smells from them rose above the roofs and reached out over the entirety of the city, attracting people from all corners. A taverna made itself known – a spindly building set in a long row – most of the tables looked to be outside and even these were filled. A bluish cloud floated above these tables, the source being a hookah that four or five middle aged men clustered around. Somehow, they managed to dodge their way inside, finding that the air itself was as coffee stained as the floor, tinged with sweet bitterness. They sat at the far corner of the dark wood bar, finally allowing the weight to be taken off their feet. When coffee arrived, Eris let her haversack fall from her shoulder. She rubbed the soreness away as Ana giggled into her cup.

"Hey, it's easier for you. You have a pair of straps."

She took a deep draught of her own drink. So much better than what we had this morning. "How far from your sister's house, do you know?"

Ana lowered an eyebrow. "Hm. Not too far, I reckon. A couple of streets away at most."

They sat and drank a while. The coffee was good, both getting in a couple more cups as the late afternoon dragged itself into the room. Ana looked progressively tenser, as though she were a clockwork mechanism wound too tight. Eris read the signal.

"Is this goodbye, then?"

"I suppose it is." Ana reached to Eris' hand, taking it softly. "Thank you."

"Whatever for?"

"For the second chance."

She withdrew, and reached to the knot keeping her *nazar*. The eye was pushed across the table and found itself staring straight at Eris.

"Oh Ana! I – "

"No, no. Take it. It must work, seeing as though it brought you to my door."

Eris took it into her palm.

"Thank you", she murmured.

They rose from their seats and embraced.

"I hope you find everything you're looking for."

"You too. Goodbye, friend Ana."

"Goodbye, Eris."

Ana leaned forward and gave her a slight kiss upon her

cheek. She then picked up her pack and left the taverna. In no time at all she had disappeared into the Larissa crowds.

Chapter Four

The taverna emptied out as the lunch hour came to an end. Eris took the opportunity to take a seat in the backmost corner. She could not face the sight of the constantly shifting crowds. The faces could not be clearly made out – they were in a state of flux, continuously changing from one to another. She was cast alone on an island in the middle of this sea, the pressure on her chest increasing bit by bit. *Perhaps I should follow Ana.* The thought was shoved to the back of her mind by a wave of tinnitus. She grabbed the left side of her head, gritting her teeth. *No. I must have the Apple. I must find Kallisti.* With that the ringing died back, stalking the back of her skull. Her thoughts would take a little time to recover.

She let the hours drift by, simply asking for refills of her coffee. Every now and then she would ask one of the many traders that wandered through for a lift. When she was denied she would sit back at her place. No one would take on a stranger. *And why should they? They had long since succumbed to cynicism, their ways cast to the* outward appearance – an odd woman asking them for a favour. This was a ruse as old as the road. A woman, a bludgeon, and a missing cart come the morning. The life of a trader, it seemed, was one of hardship and cold drachma.

Night drew on. *Heh. Some things seem to change but the distrust of people is still there. Why would I even steal a cart? I can not even drive the damn things for a start.* Eventually the sympathetic barkeep motioned to her to come to the bar. He took her to one side.

"Look", he said, "I don't want to throw you out, you seem nice enough, and I'm willing to help you out a bit. We've got a musician coming in, you see, and we could do with some help setting up. If you do that then I'll let you have one of the upstairs rooms for the night. What do you say?"

"Thank you kindly. I suppose I've got little other choice. When do you need me?"

"Oh, give it an hour."

Tables and chairs were moved outside, the exterior turning from taverna to junk shop over the course of half an hour. It was lighter work than expected – the furniture was old and cheap, and every time Eris lifted a chair she wondered whether the wickerwork would simply disintegrate in her hands. The layout was carefully reworked, the tables being left outside and the chairs arranged in a wide circle. Oil lamps were placed in an inner ring, at the feet of the front row. Their light created a ghostly, flickering stage. *This happens on a regular basis, that much is for certain. Everyone knows what goes where – what a hive I have found myself in!*

The audience began to assemble themselves; the bearded old, the smooth young, all with eyes shining excitedly in the low light. *Oh, dear Dionysus - if only you could see this! You have been forgotten, friend, long ago, but they still do as they did in Athens. Do you remember? All that is missing is the cart with your effigy riding on it. They might have forgotten the name of the City Dionysia but they still practice it. This, by all rights, is your domain. Look! They even have bearded elders who will judge the dramatic alchemy, seeing if it turns the stage into gold. We shall have to see if that happens.*

Church bells announced the coming of eleven and the crowd subdued. It was an expectant quiet, excited yet reserved, focussed on the stage. Then, a large middle-aged man with a *laoudo* strapped loosely to his body, its neck pointed downward, strode into the centre of the circle. He was in possession of a black and kept beard, with eyebrows just as bushy. There was an air of joviality about him, his portly frame telling of a man in utter comfort with himself. He craned his head up, displaying a child's smirk, and quickly surveyed the crowd before performing the best bow he could in the limited space.

"My name", he said, his voice deep, "Is Yoni Xatzhs and tonight you honour me. I can only give you my music. It is old but, there again, is it not true that music tends to become refined with age? The songs remembered are the best to sing, says I."

"That's our Yoni", the barkeep whispered to Eris. "A born showman."

"How goes the wheat Yoni?" Came a cry from the audience. Laughter followed, though the man showed no discomfort. Quite the contrary.

"Yes, yes", Yoni giggled in reply, "My trade does well. You may laugh, *kyrios Christos*, though I would make sure that my prices stay that little bit beneath your own."

There was more laughter, the heckler laughing the loudest but the performer had a hidden authority. With a quick movement of his wrist the laughter ended. Yoni's fingers touched the strings. He tapped his foot, giving himself a rhythm, and he began to play. The audience felt obliged to help and so supplied their clapping, allowing him the full movement of the stage. *He's good. Very good. An islander, I reckon.* Eris could see the waves caressing the shoreline, the other islanders readying their homes for the oncoming storm that was only just peaking over the horizon. The wind was enough of an indicator for them as it blew cold through the cypresses and buffeted the soft white dress of the new bride. His notes wove through the air, summoning this storm. As Yoni reached his crescendo it was as though rain could be felt on her skin and that the storm wind would extinguish the lanterns. He was in his element. The man issued an inner warmth as he let the *laoudo* tell its tales, a warmth that invited all around him to feel the joy he felt. There was no extreme here, no rage or consuming passion, only comfort and happiness, a simple partner who allowed the lead to be taken by others. Finally, after an hour of playing, he ceased. The music was replaced with a loud applause accompanied by the all too pleasing jangle of *drachma* on the hard wood floor.

"I say", the barkeep said. "If you're looking for a lift to Volos then he's your best bet. He goes on the regular on his round to Skiathos. You're quite lucky, in fact, as he'll be staying the night. Would you like me to ask him for you?"

"No, no. I can do that myself, thank you."

~*~

Eris awoke at six the next morning. She stirred from her bed and went about the morning routine of washing, dressing, and appraising the contents of her haversack before stepping downstairs. The place was deserted apart from the barkeep and two traders; one she did not recognise, and Yoni. He was sat alone and picked at some fatty bacon that bordered a fried egg.

"*Kalimera*", she greeted.

The man slowly turned to her. "*Kalimerasas*, miss. Were you not at the performance last night?"

"Yes. I was working off a debt. You play very well."

"Thank you. Pardon me if I appear rude but what is your business? I have a long road ahead and it is early."

"Well, I need a lift to Volos I'm on my way to Skiathos, you see."

"Hm. Well, if you like, I could take you all the way to Skiathos. That is if you do not mind two days on a donkey cart."

"I'll accept that, donkey or no. Thank you kindly."

Yoni issued a shivering yawn. "A slow donkey beats walking to Volos A two-day trip is always better than three or four."

"Haha, indeed!"

"Before I forget to ask – what is your name?"

"That would be Eris Discordia."

"Well, *kyrya Eris*, you may call me Yoni", he said, offering a hand.

"So, *kyrios Yoni*, when do we set off?"

"Oh, around eight. I might have done this run for thirty

years but I still need time to wake up."

They shook hands and Eris left him to his breakfast. *Strange man. Still, good of him to offer me a lift all the way there. Seems friendly enough. I wonder – why is he a trader rather than a musician? That's the first thing to get out of him, I suppose.* She had returned to her room, making sure that she was not leaving anything behind. Kallisti could be excused, that was stolen, but a toothbrush could not. She looked out the small window. The street, even at this time, was not completely devoid of life. Rather, early shopkeepers had flung open their doors, and a couple of food vendors had taken up residence. *I hope Ana found her sister. She's canny, though. She'll be fine.* Eris spent an hour looking at the street, watching it change from the blank expanse to being just as busy as every other in the hive of Larissa. Yoni pulled up outside.

"Hello down there!" She called.

He looked up. "Ah, I did was wondering where you had gotten to. I am ready to be off."

"Righto!"

She leapt down the stairs, giving the barkeep a quick

wave. Yoni was sat quite comfortably on his cart. It was stuffed with not only his personal luggage, which appeared to be dangling off one side, but also a great number of bulging sacks. Over all, the cart was much less rickety than she had first thought – it was old, certainly, but solidly built as far as donkey carts went. The donkey himself was more muscular than its younger brethren but looked just about as grumpy. Yoni turned to her, making the vehicle rock on its rusted springs.

"Come on up", he said, "There is enough room here on the bench."

"Thank you kindly, *kyrios Yoni*". The cart lurched as she stepped up, much to the donkey's chagrin. "Are we off?"

"Yes. This delivery is the last of the month – my day off is just over the horizon. I am quite looking forward to it. Sleep shall be had. Then it is back to the road."

He took up the reigns and the donkey, albeit begrudgingly, moved forward. *Yes, you had better move you little git.* The animal picked up some speed and joined the traffic of the city. They dodged through the crowds, making sure not to collide with any other carts. *It is an organised chaos here. One mistake and no one would be able to move.* Yet Eris was not pleased. The hot pressure of the city was taking its toll. This was the wrong kind of chaos. It was without spirit; the oppressive chains of working drudgery bore down too much. *Chaos is supposed to be freeing but it weighs us down here. It is perverted in a city. Much too planned, much too managed.* Larissa itself was not a bad place – it accepted them into its ebb and flow. Who knew what opportunity existed in one street or square? She is good. The systems that keep the city flowing, the traps and pits, were not.

Yet, for all the pessimism in Eris' mind, it took a surprisingly short time to leave. *Ah, of course. He has been doing this for years. He knows all the short cuts. Clever kyrios Yoni.* The countryside of Thessaly took them back into the oil painting. As they passed the ruins of a large stone tower the pressure relaxed, the metropolitan embrace slackening and leaving as quickly as it had appeared. She took a deep breath. Yoni laughed.

"I too feel better when I leave cities. My trade may take

me there but I much prefer the fields."

"And what trade would that be? The *laoudo* playing or the wheat?"

"Ha-ha! Which indeed. Country people appreciate the *laoudo* a little more but they tend to not be able to pay much, or do not wish to do so. With city folk nowadays it seems to be the opposite, really. If I were to stay on Skiathos I suppose I could make something, weddings and dances, but not much. And with this I get to help feed people."

"For a price."

Yoni gave her a side glance. "Ah, is that how it is? One of those Red types, eh?"

Red type?

"No, no. It all just sounds so *orderly* is all."

"Well thank goodness. Nothing spoils a nice day like politics – all too serious for the likes of me. Give me a smooth road and a new donkey. That is all I ask."

Eris grinned. *Of course.* "But what interests me, *kyrios Yoni*, is why you travel so far. Why all the way to Skiathos?"

"The same could be asked of you, *kyrya Eris*."

"Oh, absolutely. But I asked first."

"Hah! Canny – a merchant's spirit if ever I saw one. Skiathos is where me and my brothers were born. One went to war and the other to Church. I still hear from the Church – he is high up somewhere in Romania. He writes such wonderful letters and, if it is allowed, I still receive him on Christ's day which is always a joy. But yes, enough of me – tell me of you."

And Eris told him of the Apple and how far she had come so far. Yoni's look was unreadable, as though he was trying to work it all out. When Eris had finished her retelling, the merchant went quiet for a long time. Finally, he turned to her, lowering his eyebrow.

"So…you claim truly to be the goddess Eris Discordia?"

"Yes."

"And you are after your Apple?"

"Yes."

"And in all the places it could have ended up in Greece it wound up on Rhodes?"

"I detect scepticism."

"*Kyrya Eris*, I am just a trader giving you a lift. If you want to keep things close to your chest then by all means, do so. But I find it hard to believe my brother's claims about the big bearded one at the best of times – if you are a goddess you are going to have to show me."

Here we go again. She quickly raised her left hand. *Was that a flinch, kyrios Yoni?* With a flourish she proceeded to click her fingers. The sound carried down the road, bounding into the air above with a slight echo. She placed her hand back down on her lap with a vague confidence.

"Now", she said, "Something will happen. I'm not sure what but, well, *something*."

"How will we know that it was you?"

"Oh, believe me, we will know."

Yoni giggled. "If you say so, friend."

The day wore on, lazy and warm, the quiet occasionally broken by the cries of the birds that fluttered over the grassy plains from the few trees that populated that part of the world. The donkey, never one to be discouraged, would reply in grumpy tones. *Nature is its own city – just as busy and filled with denizens that wander to where they need to be. Theft and murder are an everyday occurrence and justice, the grandest chaos of all, will eventually catch up with the perpetrators.* The cart was like a boat on a gentle river, bobbing up and down with the undulations of the road, carried by its current. It drifted by a derelict farmhouse.

"I've just been thinking", Eris said, "Won't your wife be worried about you taking a strange woman all this way?"

"When did I mention a wife? I am not married."

"So, your brother is away and you're a bachelor? Is *kyrios Yoni* alone?"

"No, no. Loneliness is a very different thing to solitude. Loneliness closes you from the world - it makes you build a wall and cuts you away from all your loves and joys. Solitude is a door through which anyone can be invited. Take that farmhouse that is a lonely place, abandoned and neglected. Compare to this cart – it might be just me and a donkey but people can hope on and off as they wish.

The door to the farmhouse leads nowhere, but the seat to this cart leads to Skiathos. Or Thelassoniki, depending on the direction."

"Shall I add philosopher to the list of things *kyrios Yoni* is?"

"Ha-ha, my brother will never admit it but I read just as much as he when we were boys."

The sun had reached early evening and silence had descended, thoughtful and contemplative. Fatigue crept to their limbs and hung there. Even the donkey yawned once or twice as it went on its way. A pair of farmhands wandered by and Yoni, ever the watchful businessman, had managed to barter for their jug of beer. Apart from that intrusion they had given themselves to the conversations of nature, listening in on the gossip of the birds and the trees. *Well, she is certainly more talkative than my usual passengers. No bad thing, it must be said. Indeed, if she is the actual goddess of chaos then she is far friendlier than the title makes her out to be.* Yoni grinned.

"What're you smiling at?"

"Oh, I was just thinking. There's a spot nearby that we

can camp at. It is one I tend to use."

"Wouldn't carrying on through the night be quicker?"

"Yes, but sleep is a fine thing."

"Heh. I suppose it is."

The place of which Yoni spoke was a stony, circular patch. It was a little way off the road and had cover behind the remains of a drystone wall. Evidently it had seen a lot of use, the blackened spot in the centre told the tale of many fires that had been lit there. He stopped the cart and leapt from it, gathering the blankets as he did.

"Apologies, *kyrya Eris*, but there is no tent. It gets too humid in the summer for that. It will be stars tonight for a roof, unless you wished to try and find space amongst the wheat."

"That's fine – I have slept rough before."

"Well, it will not be so bad with the fire."

"Will you need help with that?"

"Oh, if you would not mind."

Eventually the fire was lit and a thick vegetable soup found itself bubbling in a pot above. The smell met wayward notes from Yoni's *laoudo*. Between them sat a pair of clay beakers with the remains of some of the beer glistening at the bottom. The scene was one of the utter comfort which only experienced campers can explain, a great sense of well-being and contentment. After they ate and the donkey safely tied to the nearby tree they hunkered down for the night.

"*Kyrios Yoni*", Eris yawned, "Why didn't we camp in that farmhouse? It's just over the hill."

"I have no wish to disturb any ghosts tonight."

Chapter Five

The night had been a strange one. When the pair had set themselves to sleep a deep fog had descended, circling around the light of the fire. As the fire gently died it tightened itself around them, like a snake readying its coils. There was no source for this fog, no stream or pool – it seemed to drift from the ground itself in long and spectral fingers. It moved without a breeze, drifting under its own power. What intelligence it had was nothing short of malicious. Finally, it saw its chance to strike. The darkness had covered Eris' head, making it the perfect target. Grabbing claws punched through the air only to silently explode soundlessly. The *nazar*, that ever watching lookout, stared at the fog. For a moment the fog stared back. Then it retreated, sinking back into the ground.

"Serves you right too", Eris mumbled.

Yoni continued to snore.

~*~

Yoni rose with the sun, twisting his back. Grunting, he

looked to the dark horizon. *Rain in a couple of hours. Best get things ready.* He yawned, and padded over to the cart, taking out a large piece of hide. The donkey groaned when he saw it. *Yes, yes, you hate your coat. But you know that it is better than being cold and drenched.* He returned to the cart to get the breakfast things, hunkered down and relit the fire. As the bacon quietly sizzled he let his eyes wander to Eris' sleeping form. *She certainly is an odd one. Really think she's Eris. Ah well, as my mother always said – "By the grace of God on High". She's no harm. Let her live as she will. God knows we could learn to do that in these days. With any luck, she will get where she needs to be.* He annoyed the bacon, making it hiss. *I had better wake her.*

"*Kalimera, kyrya Eris*", he said.

She yawned awake. "*Kalimerasas, kyrios Yoni*"

"I do apologise for waking you so early but there is a storm coming. Breakfast is just about done."

"Excellent", said she.

What is excellent, kyrya Eris? The storm or breakfast?

It took them half an hour to finish breakfast and quickly

wash. Soon after setting off, that slowness which marked the day before returned, settling on the creaking wheels. They had all the time they needed to make the journey and breathed easy. Insects sang through the air, chased closely by birds which darted on by. Here and there labourers made their way to the fields, the thumping of their tools adding percussion to the silence. After a couple of hours went by Yoni leapt from the cart.

"What're you doing?" Eris asked.

"I would like to strum on the *laoudo* for a while", he replied. "Do you mind?"

"Not at all."

He leapt back to his seat, instrument strapped to him.

"I say", he said as he picked at the strings, "Did something happen last night?"

Eris thought carefully. "No."

"Odd. I have quickly left that place occasionally because, well, it felt wrong."

He went back to busying himself with the *laoudo*, leaving Eris to chase her thoughts all the way to Rhodes. *What will I do when I get there? If I asked my family they would cry vengeance, no doubt. The little guttersnipe does deserve something. What could my rage possibly create? Who even thinks of stealing from the gods themselves? There's one odd thing, though. This person should be the richest in Greece. Yet no one knows him. With riches comes fame, after all. But still: stealing from a deity is rather like steering a ship straight toward the lighthouse – begs for rocks.* She sank into her seat. *I wonder, though.*

"So…has anything happened, yet?"

Yoni bunched his brow. "No. I don't think so."

"I suppose I'm getting rusty."

"Ha-ha! That's what happens as we get older!"

"Old? I'm a goddess!"

"Then you're older than most."

Damn. Good point. He's still joking. Humouring me. He doesn't believe me in the slightest. Yet he still wants to do me a good turn. What a strange man.

"You don't believe me when I say that, do you?"

Yoni faced her. "I tell you, *kyrya Eris*, that what I believe is what I believe. That does not matter to anyone other than myself. I could tell you that I believe you absolutely but why would that matter? What I think does not affect you one way or the other."

"But what do you think?"

The trader made his considerations carefully. *How do I word this?*

"There is...something about you, I suppose. I am no poet. I cannot tell you exactly what I mean by that. But, admittedly, there is something about you."

"That is quite vague, *kyrios Yoni*. It could be said about anyone."

"Heh. Yes, well, I'm not a writer. Though, when we get to Skiathos I will introduce you to my friend Alexandros. Old man but a prolific writer. I reckon that you would like him."

As the cart climbed to the top of a hill the wind suddenly picked up. Invisible hands grabbed at the floor and picked up small stones and long dead leaves. The hands then began to gently pelt the side of the cart and the donkey. The animal responded with its usual protestations toward the world around it. Looking up, Yoni could see that the clouds were moving in and were ready to burst.

They were grey and heavy, scraping themselves along the tops of the higher hills in the distance. *Just as I thought. The rain should start in a bit.* He silently thanked the cart's roof that hung over the seat. It had held up for many years before – his passenger and himself would remain reasonably dry. The air felt like a fog bank, growing in dampness. *If we are lucky it ought to come down as a drizzle. If unlucky then I hope that the cart floats.*

Then the rain began. It began as a series of sudden thuds. Then it became a torrent. In a matter of minutes, the world had become a washed-out watercolour.

"Is this your doing?" Yoni grinned.

"Perhaps. As I say – I'm never quite sure what will happen when events are set in motion."

Yoni shook his head, his grin wide. Whenever he encountered rain like this it always made him glad at heart. It had a pleasing sound, one that allowed him to think of nothing, washing his mind of detritus just as it cleaned the road. He settled back in his seat. Eris, however, looked furtively about. *It is just a storm. It cannot be anything else. No. I have summoned some rain* is all. *Not the worst, but I will probably have to pay extra for the room, being wet and all. Fair enough. Mild inconvenience. Nothing dramatic. All is well.* She emulated Yoni, trying to relax. *Soon I will be on the ferry to Skiathos. Not an island I have been to very often. Lemnos, Crete, but not Skiathos. Oughtn't be that bad, really.*

"Would you like a blanket? It has just dropped cold", Yoni offered.

"No, no. I quite like the cold."

"Do you mind if I get one?"

"By all means."

"Thank you kindly."

Such an odd thing. Why did he have to ask on his own cart? Humans are such strange things when all is said. They know for a fact that they cannot defeat the elements. Of course, they can guard against them and aggravate them to an extent but they cannot control them. They are islands of order in the ocean of chaos, it seems. Always, they want to be strong so they share their weaknesses. A weakness shared is no weakness at all – it allows for the requisite amount of discord to exist without being too jarring. Still, he doesn't believe. If he did then he would never have offered me a blanket – cold doesn't affect the gods. Why can they never take anything at face value?

The answer came in the form of a lightening flash and a long peal of thunder.

"Oh-ho!" Yoni exclaimed. "The storm lives!"

He patted himself down, finding his pipe and filling it with his cheap tobacco.

"Can you fill mine?" Eris asked, taking her own pipe from her pack.

"Absolutely. Careful, though. This is not the best stuff. It will burn your chest like Icarus' wings."

Eris giggled. "That doesn't bode well in the slightest, *kyrios* Yoni."

Foul, blue smoke joined the rain. With every moment, the thunder and lightning was coming closer. We should be fine. There are a couple of trees taller than us hereabout. The stillness of yesterday had all but disappeared, lost to the electric atmosphere. The donkey replied to each peal, honking in anger. The ground had become the drum for the rain, hitting a strange rhythm, unfollowable, incomprehensible. The land was too thirsty to protest and gladly accepted the wine from above, quenching its weeks burning throat. Indeed, the trees danced in reverie of this storm as their roots moved with the effort to drink as much as they could. There was a loud clap, louder than any that had sounded before, and even the donkey quailed. They were under the storm now, its complete focus. Eris shifted uneasily. She could feel that something weird was at work – this was not an ordinary storm.

"I should not worry", Yoni stated. "The trees are still taller than we. Trees are better targets – they smoke much better than a cart can."

No. These are father's bolts. The aim is too right. He's angry at something and has chosen to scour the Earth of whatever it is. And of anything which gets in the vicinity, as a matter of course. But that's the thing. He's angry but he won't know what he's angry at. Too far gone for far too long. She was about to speak up when, as keen as Achilleus' spear flying into Trojan Hektor, a bolt struck the donkey. The poor animal had no time to make a single sound. The force rocked the cart. The crater smoked in front of them. Yoni's reigns cut off after five inches. The cheap tobacco was drowned by cooked meat. Neither wanted to look. Yoni slowly turned to Eris.

"Well", he said, "you did say that something would happen."

~*~

The storm took an hour to pass. To attempt to escape the smell of cooked donkey they clambered to the back of the cart, saying little as Yoni dug around for his shovel. He found it just as the lightening died. As they re-emerged there was still a light drizzle, though negligible.

"At least the ground is soft with the rain", he said. "It will make things easier."

"Do you need any help?"

He stroked his beard. "Oh no, *kyrya Eris*, this is not the work for the likes of yourself."

At first he looked at both sides of the road. To the left was a hedgerow, a verge to the right. He sighed, crossing to the verge and starting the dig. Eris watched from the cart, noticing that the contented light that had hitherto crowned him was nowhere to be seen. With every heavy shovelful, he gave a loud grunt. He knows I'm a goddess now. He knows but still treats me as an ordinary woman. No bowing, no deference. Such a strange man. Finally, the grave was dug. He made his way to the crater but halted at the edge. Come on. You have seen worse than a cooked donkey. The smell still lingered slightly in the air despite the rainfall, making his nose wrinkle up. Yet he still managed to drag out the remains. A charred torso, its legs sticking rigidly out, was all that was left. Not even the tail had survived. Goodness – father must've been very angry. Yoni dumped the corpse into its new home in silence. He winced at the sight of the dirt pile

"Actually, could you help me with the dirt? It would be much appreciated."

"Of course."

"There is another shovel in the back."

Between them it took no time to complete the job. With what was left over they filled in the hole in the road. There was no evidence of the event. Yoni sighed.

"How will we get to Volos?" Asked Eris.

"There are two options, in my experience. We could pull the cart ourselves, though the last time I did that I was a much younger man, or we could wait till another cart passes by."

"How well used is this road?"

He gave a sharp intake of breath. "After a storm like that? I would say that we should see traffic tomorrow. Tonight, even, if they have set off from Larissa early enough. But not for a long while irregardless."

Eris sighed. The chilly air embraced them, sharing its remaining moisture which dripped from the sleeves of her blouse and hem of her mud splattered dress. Yoni shivered. Christ – I hate storms. Even when they supposed to have gone they just do not go away. He relit his pipe and did the same with hers.

"We will sleep on the cart tonight. The ground is too wet. It will have to be the dried meat for tonight and the morning"

"That's fine. Sorry about the donkey"

Yoni Xatzhs was a man who was well within his

element on the road, just as much as the marketplace. The look he wore told as much – a deep working out was occurring. The man puffed a few times on his pipe. A merchant's scales are an invisible tool – the ones seen on the stand are not the ones they use. Rather, they are used so much over the course of a merchant's life that they become an external organ. Merchants always know what is worth what at any given time and not all prices can be seen in terms of drachma. What is he reckoning up? He shook his head twice in as many minutes as various mental transactions failed. When the scales tipped into their equilibrium, however, it was very much visible. It could be seen on his face – he had finally found a transaction that worked, a deal that could be made. He looked at her, eyes shining.

"Well, if you want to atone for my loss, I have a deal for you. If, of course, you want it."

She looked at him, unsure. A deal? Has this man never heard of what happens to those who try to deal with the likes of us? Where is this going?

"What is this deal?"

"No need to be defensive, *kyrya Eris*, it is completely equitable. I merely wish to ask you a question. I am a curious man by nature."

"And what question would that be? About the nature of chaos? The secret of discord? Heavy questions lead to heavy answers, friend Yoni. I've seen intelligent people fall to insanity trying to comprehend the things I have chosen to tell them. However, if you really do wish to ask me such a question do please ask it."

Yoni was taken aback. "I ask nothing so grandiose. I only want to know why you pursue the Apple so. You know all about me so I believe that it should be reciprocal. Tell me about your journey."

"Oh, that. Yes. Much more sensible…On where I begin depends on how much you know about the Apple already"

"Nothing. I was not taught such things."

Eris nodded. "It's a long tale."

"We will be having a long wait."

He settled into his seat on the cart and motioned for her to begin.

"I created it aeons ago. Back then I was still a young

goddess and thought of plans and means to cause chaos. I think that you can see how that is somewhat ridiculous. The Apple was a part of one of those schemes. I formed a game – that whomever between Hera, Aphrodite, and Athena was named the most beautiful would win it. Of course, they began to argue and fight. It was all…quite amusing. They approached a human prince, Paris of Troy, and tried to bribe him into selecting one of them. As gods are often wont to do Athena and Hera underestimated the power of human sexuality. He chose Aphrodite. Seeing as though she presented him with Helen of Sparta I cannot possibly blame him. To cut a long, weary, story short this caused the Trojan War.

"It's something of an unwritten rule that gods, deities in general, have some kind of symbol. When you think of Athena you think of the Owl, Poseidon his Trident. Those symbols let us live on, live far beyond our actual forms. This particular one", Eris gestured to herself, "Is quite different from the one that came before. But it is deeper than that. My Apple is as much as a part of me as your left arm is a part of you. Its removal is just as distressing and, yes, I do feel the same pain that a missing limb would give. I choose not to show it – that is weakness in the eyes of mortals."

Yoni exhaled. "And that is why you chase it?"

"Yes."

He considered it all for a moment. "Showing pain is not a weakness, friend."

"Oh?"

"No. It makes you seem more human, I think. But what I do not understand is why you do not make another."

"Ah, well, it simply wouldn't be the same. It wouldn't be *Kallisti*."

"I think I see. Thank you for telling me."

"You're welcome. Did it repay you for the donkey?"

"Yes. To its exact value."

"Excellent."

They sat back, puffing away at their pipes. The afternoon moved to early evening. Luckily, after some rummaging, Yoni found some kindling that had remained dry. He built a small fire, boiled a kettle on it, and made them coffee. The birds that had evacuated the area before the storm had returned, their chattering lessening the feelings of loneliness and melancholy. Even the insects had made a return. Life was making a comeback after the storm, surrounding them completely. The storm was a random event, nothing more than a blip of chaos in the natural order of the world. That same order had returned. It always did. Truly, order is simply a part of the web of chaos – it is the object that sits in the centre, the thing which the rest of the web is built around. Without order, chaos would break down and be left flapping in the breeze. Indeed, what are rules if they cannot be broken? The rules of chaos must be broken just as often as the rules of order. Even I've got rules to abide by, limits to adhere to. Yet humans refuse their limits, as obvious as they are. Most gods would've gone into a sheer rage at being asked such a question. But there is nothing, absolutely nothing, that is as harmless and yet ultimately as harmful.

They spent the rest of the evening engaged in idle talk. Yoni built up the fire, hoping to signal anyone who might pass by. It was not until midnight, when the constellations were in full regalia, that the truck came bounding down the road. Yoni had flagged it down and, after a little haggling, managed to get the cart hitched to the back. They were on the way to Volos.

Chapter Six

The truck driver, whose name was Ioannis, was a man considerably thinner than Yoni. Under his red nose was a thick black moustache, well maintained, and his clothes, though hardy, could be described as neat. He was surrounded with the smell of cheap chewing tobacco that settled strong in the cramped environ of the truck cab. As the truck leapt along the midnight road the back jingled with bottles of *tsipouro* tightly packed into straw filled crates. In a day they would find themselves in the bars and clubs of Volos.

"When they want a supplier", Ioannis croaked, "they come to me. I'm sure you understand, Yoni."

"Yes. People in Skiathos like my ways."

"Ha! Volos likes the fact that I don't keep bottles back!"

His truck was a dirty, noisy thing but undeniably new. Eris looked to Yoni when he first saw it. He had visibly shrunk. *Even now power is something to be flaunted. The tyrants of Athens may have gone but the power of wealth remains the same. Ioannis is a lord. An unspoken ruler in his small kingdom of the market. A nasty little man, really.* When she had told him the tale of the donkey the younger man's laugh mimicked the dead animal, slapping Yoni heartily on his back with a loud thump. *Well. I'm glad to be sat at the window. Good idea, kyrios Yoni, good idea.* The two men strapped the donkey cart to the back of the truck, making sure that the ropes were tight.

As she looked out the window, trying all she could not to meet Ioannis' little eyes, the hedgerows and silhouetted trees, the stars themselves, disappeared into the black. *It's as though the world is painted on a curtain that is being pulled away. There is no window behind – behind the curtain there is nothing.* However, the truck began to slow. The jingling bottles were quieting, and Yoni's trailer finally settled, ceasing its relentless jumps over the ruts and holes in the road. He sighed with relief. *With luck, the cargo will be in one piece.* Houses appeared as they slowed into the outskirts of a small town. Ioannis yawned deeply. It seemed that the only thing keeping him in the waking world was the sheer noise of the truck's engine. It suddenly ceased.

"We could all do with a rest, so I reckon", Ioannis said as he leapt from his seat. "I don't know about you but I've been driving since the crack of dawn. If I go any further I'll be as dead as your donkey."

Yoni grumbled. "I suppose we could stop now. But, surely, nowhere will be open?"

"Ah – this place is always open for me. Come, friends."

As they fell behind, Eris gave Yoni a sly look.

"What?"

"You don't like this man, do you?" She said, voice low.

As she spoke Ioannis spat a thick, brown globule to the ground, quickly wiping at his moustache.

"Of course not."

They stayed overnight at a small hostel and the next morning indulged in a meagre breakfast, paid for by Yoni. The Sun was still low when they left for Volos The arrangement of the cab was the same as the day before, with Ioannis driving and Eris at the far window. *He's uncomfortable with that. He wanted me to be next to him.*

Horrid little man. Speed and time. The two are connected. The more speed there is, the less time there is. On the cart, there was all the time we needed – the slowness of the journey granted us weeks, years, to get to Volos But here time is crushed into a can, chopped into tiny chunks to be eaten all in one gulp. We must get to Volos as quickly as possible. Time turns from friend to enemy, ally to rival. We now must defeat it, cast it away. Eris sighed. Before now, the trip had been a meandering creature. Unlike the time she had spent amongst her brethren, static in the kingdoms of Heaven. It was difficult to even breathe under the aegis of her senile, ageing father. Yet in that truck the air was being taken from her again. *Speed is the acid that dissolves distance. A slow cart drifts over the distance – a truck cuts through it. The river of time, once so unstoppable, has found a dam and is only allowed to flow with the slightest permission given.* She sunk her head down. *Progress is the synthesis of chaos and order – it is chaos directed to an unseen goal.*

After two or three hours of driving they finally passed by the first few buildings of Volos The road had turned from being moderately rough to fully paved, lined in the middle with rail tracks. The traffic, that before had been light at best, had built up very quickly. There was a feeling of youth about the place – this was new, popping up out of nowhere and sprawling, powered by the sea which it embraced. Yet the buildings were still little more than white and orange blurs as the truck sped into town. The only thing that slowed it was the other traffic. Then houses, shops, churches, and warehouses came into being. Finally, the world had found its form once again.

"We'll have to be careful as we get to the seafront", said Ioannis, "Seems to be a busy day today."

Eris was still lost in her thoughts. *It might think itself new but cities never really change. They remain cauldrons of insanity – everyone trying to get somewhere for some reason. It is a great collision of anything and anyone where anything can happen. Merely going to market becomes an adventure. You wanted a bunch of apples and, suddenly, you are on a ship bound for Constantinople, pressed ganged to a life on the sea. The buildings change, the mix of people is in constant shift and tipping their balances in one way or another, but the cauldron remains the same.* Suddenly, a shrill whistle cut through the truck which suddenly hefted left.

"Do look where you are going!" Yoni cried.

"Hey – I'm helping you out!"

"Ogling the women on the side of the road helps no one!"

She left the men to argue, electing instead to look at the machine coming toward them. It was a box around the size of the truck. However, a rounded cylinder jutted out of the front and, in turn, was topped with a short pipe spewing black smoke. It moved fluidly over the rails, pulling a load of goods behind it. As the steam engine sailed by, she felt a wave of optimism. *How clever they are! That funny little bearded man always said that steam would power machines one day. That was when he wasn't too busy playing with his gears, that is. Certainly took them a while.* The last train car rattled by, leaving them to get to the end of its own journey. *I wonder where it's going. Can't ask those two – shouting at each other like Athena and Aphrodite. How strange that they are so concerned with themselves that they cannot seem to accept that the world at large, well, doesn't exactly care. It will carry on irregardless of how the argument ends.*

For the final half hour the truck was bathed in silence. As they approached the seafront the buildings became ever older, yet the air was still tinged with the sharp taste of progress. It was all over the city – the people lived in the midst of it, building railways, docks, and factories to give them more of that taste. Its sharpness is the same as that found in a cup of mint tea, offset with an addictive sweetness. *These buildings will not be standing here for long. Like all other things here they will be broken down and rebuilt, changed as the times demand them. But still the city will remain the same. Still it will be Volos, young and leaping Volos* Ioannis drove the truck into a snicket between a coffee-shop and a haberdashery.

"Right", he said, "This ought to be a safe enough spot for you to keep your wares. Unless, of course, you wished to pull it to the ferry yourself."

Yoni gave him a side-eyed glance. "No. Here will do."

They got out and Yoni unhooked his cart. "Thank you

for taking us this far."

"Not a problem", Ioannis replied. He held his hand out. Yoni paid him a ten *drachma* note. "Ah, this ought to cover costs quite nicely. I hope that you and your…lady friend…get to where you need to go. *Andíl.*"

His eyes flicked up and down Eris' body. With a tight, toothy grin he leapt to the front of the truck, turning the crank handle.

"What do you think he meant by that?" Eris asked.

"Some men seem to think that all that men and women can do is share a bed."

"I thought as much."

As the *tsipouro* merchant left the alleyway in a cloud of black smoke she held a hand behind her back and gave her fingers a click. *I shan't know what happens to him. But it's damned cathartic.*

"He will come to a bad end, I expect", Yoni stated. "Too…too flash. Too quick with his words, that one. His thoughts can never catch up."

"I quite agree, *kyrios Yoni.*"

The coffee-shop next door was a bright affair. The

tables were of dark wood, the waiters all but ran from table to counter with their aprons flapping through the coffee scented fog. The pair were thankful to see that all the seats were padded. When they sat, it was a marked improvement from the seats in the truck, though the stiffness in their spines and legs still did its awful work. It was apparent, however, that the coffee they were served was meant for quick consumption rather than dwelling upon. Downing a gulp, Yoni could not suppress his grimace.

"Hah! Makes you wish for the stuff on the road, does it not?"

"Hm. That it does."

They drank it slowly regardless. According to the wall clock it was only nine, and the ferry would not leave for another hour or so by Yoni's reckoning. *The sea looks still enough. Ought not be a bad trip for her.*

"*Kyrya Eris*, may I just say that it has been a delight to have you on my cart. The trip to Volos is often a lonely one. I am glad to have shared it with a friend."

"I thank you for taking me this far. Most wouldn't have

bothered at all. But how much do I owe you?"

Yoni waved a hand. "Ah, it is fine. Keep your money for Skiathos. It may be my home, but I must say that there are those who charge too much for things. I am quite happy to have gained a friend – that is profit enough for me."

"Why, *kyrios Yoni*, are you getting all soft?"

"No. I will be sure to forward you a bill for the new donkey."

He chuckled as he took another sip of his coffee. *He is quite an odd one. A merchant with no money, and no care for it. And a friend? I suppose so. Ana too...in a way...*

"When shall we go to the quayside?" She asked.

"Oh...after coffee. I am not used to so much moving nowadays. Events are always happening in these strange times. Makes a man want to sit still for a while."

"Ha. I can attest to that."

They finished their coffee and, after a brief and heated discussion, Yoni paid. There was not that much distance from the coffee-shop to the quayside yet it felt as though it took a long time to cross the road there. *Truly, exiting the stage is the slowest movement of the actor.* When they reached the pier the ferry bounced like an excited horse in a stable. The boat was a glorified tug. *Looks like everything else – old, reliable, and slightly shaky.*

"Will that be my vessel?"

"Yes. I am only sorry that I could not come along with you. But still, if you mention my name around the place then you should be able to get along well enough. I am, if I might say so, well liked on the island."

They stood on the dock, looking up at the boat. Yoni turned to her.

"Thank you", he said, "For asking me for your favour. I think, though, that the time has come. *Yiassas, kyrya Eris.* Until we bump into each other on another strange road."

"*Yiassas, kyrios Yoni.* May the winds of chaos guide you further on yours."

She crossed the gangplank and took a spot on the keel, looking back on the town. *Mortals are strange beings to say the least. You never quite know what it is they're up to.* The tug yelled out, the gangplank was raised. As the boat began to move Yoni raised his hand, grinning wide.

"For the Apple!"

Chapter Seven

The sea is, ultimately, a deceptive thing. It is a flat, wide desert of darkest blue. But dip a hand under the surface, lift it to your face and what do you find? It turns invisible, the colour fading away. There are secrets here, buried deep at the bottom. Even the lord of the seas himself can never decipher what it is thinking of, what it hides in the trenches and crevasses. It does not like being one thing or the other, constantly shifting from one state to another. When a sailor says that the sea is calm it will suddenly change from blue to grey and build to vast towers that will come crashing upon the decks and cabins, dashing them to watery oblivion. We are mere toys in the realm of nature.

As for the crossing to Skiathos it was rather uneventful. The ferry was crowded. Many traders were there, staying close to their carts though some islanders, most of whom women, had found themselves clustered around the bowsprit. They held firm to their shopping baskets and bundles. One tried all that she could to control a loud, obnoxious chicken. Yet Eris, even amongst this hubbub, found a fragile peace. The overpowering song of the waves nullified the persistent ringing in her ears, and the salt in the air acted as a balm on her aching chest. *The chaos of the sea is different from that of the city. The city is always a spectacle, always in one's face. But the sea has an invisible anarchy about it, the spectacle is rare and, often, years in the making.* It took a couple of hours to reach the island.

The little tug docked at the quayside, rocking gently against it. As the passengers walked down the gangplank they paid the captain his dues. The carts were wheeled off first, followed by the beasts that pulled them, and then the people. *How can such a little port be so busy?* It was every bit as active as Volos Shouts and talk were all around, and little clouds of pipe smoke erupted to join it. As soon as her feet met the cobbles the tightness in her chest came back, doubling what it was before, making her clutch the *nazar* that dangled there. *Steady. I'm moving. Must find Kallisti. I can't stay here long, that's for sure. I had hoped to get to Rhodes before this happened. Plans aren't my thing, I suppose.* She walked into town. *Right, what was the name of that writer? Alexandros? That's it!*

She wandered down a narrow street, coming to a small bar. It was full of men hunkered over the tables, keeping to low voices. Eris could sense not only the presence of Posideon but of Ares – violence had touched these men. The proprietor, stood behind the bar, was just as scruffy as the rest of building.

"*Kalispera!* Would you know where I could find Alexandros Papadiamantis? I was told that he could help me with something?"

"The old priest? I can tell you – you need to take the next street over, about halfway up. He's been ill for a while, though. Can't tell you if he's well enough to talk or anything. Good man, I think. Every man in here could tell you that."

"Thank you for your help."

"Not a problem."

She placed a drachma in the tip jar and left the place. By now the light had turned into the dusk amalgam of orange and pink. A couple of lamplighters were efficiently taking care of their business and people were making their way back to their little homes after the day's goings on. Eris made her way through the terraces until, finally, she came by the house. It was a little larger than the others, though not imposing, fitting snugly in the row. She could just make out a hunched form of a man looking over a desk on the upper balcony.

"*Kyrios Papadiamantis!*" She called.

"Come in", came his voice, "You will easily find your way up. Anyone is welcome here."

Eris crossed the threshold and was faced with a corridor with stairs leading up. She climbed the stair and found herself in the writer's bedroom and crossed to the balcony. *Better not interrupt. There's nothing quite so wrathful than an artist disturbed.* Alexandros was dressed all in black, his neck covered in a high collar. He was pale and quite thin, though one could tell that he had once been well built. His eyes were ringed, peaking over an impressive moustache that threatened to drape over his top lip, focussed on the paper set before him as his pen was arthritically dragged over its surface. *Has he even noticed me? He's not even that old! Ana was older. Something's wrong, I think.*

"Sorry...I'll be right with you...just finishing a paragraph. Do please sit."

She sat. *There's no need to disturb anything – art is its own chaos, after all.* She looked out over the street, down toward the port, and watched the little boats hauled up the slope and the darkness of the sea. The whole town was glowing with street-lights. As the lamplighters made their way toward the house Alexandros gave them a wave without even looking up. Laughter echoed up the street, followed by a gang of youths, arm in arm. Rather than any perturbation there was instead a slight grin on his face. *I wonder what he's writing. So preoccupied, it seems.* Finally, he put the pen down and sat back in his wicker chair to look at her.

"Ah, sorry. I do so hate leaving things unfinished. I suppose that you might be the same."

"What do you mean?"

The old man lifted his left hand weakly and gave his fingers a click. "Am I right?"

"Y-yes. How –"

"I have been waiting for you for quite a while now. I think I know what it is you are looking for."

"And what would that be, oh great detective?"

"Heh. That would be your Apple."

Eris' eyes widened.

"When did you see it?"

"Oh, when I was ten years old. Shall I tell you the tale?"

"Please."

"Very well. My father was a priest. He, like me, kept this house open to all who needed shelter. One day I had come back from school and was in the parlour when, suddenly, a haggard looking man came bounding through the door. He was young – twenties I would say. Well, he tried speaking to me in English, quick and panicking. This was a man in trouble, I thought, and so I called for my father. He was at study and could not help but show some amount of annoyance. But once he got the straight tale out of me he rose from his chair to greet the Englishman. When he approached, the man all but embraced his legs!

He was nearly weeping. My father placed a hand on his shoulder and comforted him, ordering me to quickly get some water. As I was about to leave the room something fell from his pack – it thudded across the floor and stopped just short of my feet. It was a bundle, quickly and badly wrapped. The man shouted and grabbed it, shoving it to the bottom of his bag.

"He stayed with us for two days, only calming properly at dinner. My father had that effect on people – not this big man preaching of damnation, but quiet and calm. He was thoughtful and made others think. I do not reckon that this man's head had been so clear for many days. We learned that his name was Malcolm and that he was indeed an Englishman come to write of our fair country. He wrote off his apparent madness as being nothing more than a bad case of the heat stroke and that he was becoming well again. As with every diligent ten-year old I did not trust this one iota. We had all sorts come into the house at that time, of course, but this Malcolm was the one that I never took to liking. Something wrong with his eyes, I think. But yes, I was also quite nosy. When I got the chance, I managed to peak into the spare room, where we were keeping him. And that's where I saw it."

"Kallisti?"

"Yes. My dear, if I may say so, it was one of the most beautiful things I have ever seen."

"Well, that is the thing's name sake."

Alexandros laughed. "Indeed. It was sat on his bed, an apple of purest gold emblazoned with a black letter *K*. It was only a glimpse, short and passing. This Malcolm suddenly slammed the door before I could get any more of a look, though I do not think he noticed me. When I placed my head to the door I could hear him muttering, you see. Something about thievery, safety, keeping hidden. But that is all I can remember. I still dream of the Apple, *kyrya Eris*. It is not the kind of thing that leaves one's memory. Like a little sun in my mind it remains shining."

"It's in Rhodes. I knew that much. But the name – that was what I needed. Thank you, friend."

"That is quite alright. You are welcome to stay here for as long as you need. The next ferry will be tomorrow morning and, from here, it takes two days over the Aegean. Quite a way out, is Rhodes."

Eris was about to reply when the dam finally broke. The ringing in her ears turned into a screech, weighing her head down, all but shoving it to the table. As it dipped she thrust her arm forward, keeping herself from slamming it on the surface. Her chest squeezed. Her breathing was heavy. *Not now! So close!* The world moved up and down and turned quickly about her. She could barely hear. Suddenly, there came a feeling of a gentle hand on her shoulder and the barest sensation of standing. Colours blurred into each other, the mess overlaid with speckles of light. Sound was non-existent apart from that long ring. A feeling of a hard mattress beneath her.

It was as though she had run to the quay and thrown herself into the ocean. She could not find solid ground as she was pushed by the currents of the onslaught, a pendulum swinging wild in the wind. When she opened her eyes the world was distorted. There were no shapes that she could make out, and the colours all existed in the dark yellows and browns. Thought was shattered. Single words, letters, floated to the top and were quickly drowned again. There was a piece missing, an important rope, the keystone, the nail. She was unravelling, spinning away from the loom and into darkness. Finally darkness. What was this? Death? No. No bemused looking Hades was looking down at her. Sleep? No. Sleep, even comfortable sleep, is more fitful than this. Darkness gave way to blue. A green spot in the blue appeared and grew into an island, a tiny canvas unfolding. Rhodes. The northern part of the island came into focus. A feeling of falling. A small house standing alone near the sea. Fishnets piled on a boat outside. On a chair on the edge an old fisherman. He turns and says one word.

"Kallisti."

And darkness fell again.

~*~

Eris sighed. Bleary eyed, she tried to get up only for a wall of dizziness to meet her on the way. She flopped back down. Slowly turning her head, she saw that there was a bedside table fashioned with a large jug of water and some bread. She reached across. *Hungry. No food yet. Water first.* She gulped it down, the dizziness beginning to melt away. *Better. Try again?* She got up, slowly this time, and sat still. *Still dizzy. Not as bad, though.* Taking deep breaths, she took stock of her situation. *First of all – morning has broken. That means that I have been out all night. Right. Might've missed the ferry. Second – I need a wash. Third – things are worse than I had first thought. I must get Kallisti as soon as possible.*

Getting to her feet she could hear a slight chanting coming from downstairs. *What?* She left the room and followed the sound down the stairs and through a door to the right. It was a quaint little parlour, sparsely furnished. On one end was a table on which sat a crucifix and a candle. Alexandros was knelt before it, hands tenting against his face. His chanting was soft, the rhythm hidden in the low volume. *Priests. If merchants are strange then priests are odder.* As she stepped forward he stopped and slowly turned.

"Oh! I do apologise! Did I disturb your rest?"

"No, no. I woke on my own accord."

"Oh good. Are you feeling better?"

"I don't think that I'm going to get much better without the Apple, I'm afraid."

"Yes, yes, of course. Well, I can tell you that you were passed out for two days. However, today you are in luck. The ferry does not leave for Rhodes for two hours yet and, better yet, there is time for breakfast."

Breakfast was small but filling. Afterwards, Eris washed and changed into a new blouse and skirt, casting the soiled clothes of the road to the very bottom of her bag. The time for leaving came quickly. Alexandros was at the door, holding it patiently.

"Well, thank you for letting me stay."

"You are very welcome, *kyrya Eris*. Please, if you ever come by this part of the world again, do not hesitate to knock on my door. Perhaps I will have finished my writings by then and you will be in better spirits."

"Yes, I think I will."

With that she bade him farewell and walked back to the quay. There another ferry, larger than the one from Volos, was waiting. The captain was stood taking fares as people boarded. He doffed his cap as she joined them. So, for the second time, she entered the realm of the enigmatic Aegean.

Chapter Eight

The fragile peace of the Skiathos crossing had shattered on the deck. Eris paced up and down, only stopping to peek at the horizon for the elusive Rhodes. Her world was noise, her mind spinning in a vortex of clashing sound. *Two days. I can last two more days. All I've got to do is focus on the Apple. Kallisti is a couple day's hike away – not long at all.* When she sat her leg jiggled to the rhythm of its own music. Not since the beginning of her sleep did she feel this way – a restless, exhausting agitation.

The ferry was completely different in cargo than the last. It was exclusively human, with not a single animal to be seen. She stayed well away from them, within earshot. It was a calming thing to listen to the absent chatter of the peasants – their problems were so Earthly, so normal. Matters of marriage and agriculture floated by. Indeed, her ears pricked up when she overheard one anecdote from a woman visiting Volos

"Yes – I tell you true!" She exclaimed. "I saw it happen myself. The man had just parked up his truck on the quayside and gotten out when there was a loud pop, there's no other way of describing it, and the machine started rolling backwards and straight off the pier. The man was chasing the damned thing right to the very end, let me tell you. When I last saw him, he was just stood there on the edge of the dock, staring at the spot where the truck was lost. Being a compassionate woman, I did feel some sympathy but there's very little one can do…"

And the talk went on. Eris could not help but feel a certain satisfaction about the news. *I bet thirty drachmae that the "poor man" was a tsipouro merchant.* When it came to midday that same woman opened a basket she was carrying and shared the bread and fish within around the boat. Eris gratefully took some and was about to pay her.

"No, no", the woman said with a hand aloft. "I'm a cook by profession. What good's cooking when no one can enjoy it – money makes the food much too bitter."

There came a call from the stern. "How about me?"

"You've got quite enough yourself!"

"Oh! That's all I get for my services! Woe is me!"

"And here I thought your name was Nikos!"

The afternoon went about its weary way, hours passing by as the nautical miles were tread. Eris sat alone. The others were so engrossed in their lives that they all looked through the strange young woman on the aft bench. *Kallisti was stolen fifty years ago. Fifty! Why did it take so long for me to notice? I should've taken it with me when we left. But everyone else left their things. I suppose they were hidden well. But still! This should never have happened.* She leaned forward, cradling her head in her hands. *I've been away too long. I can't go back. There's too much to be done. Something is in the air. Something big. We aren't even in discord. At this point it is simple ridiculousness.* She shook her head. *That's not even the problem, though. Kallisti was never meant for mortals. It sends gods mad for goodness' sake! How Rhodes is still even there at all is beyond me.*

The sea lapped at the side of the boat, an attentive observer to the proceedings. It looked to be clearer than usual, the sun taking away the already negligible opacity. Swarms of silver coloured fish made themselves known, gently embracing the boat on their way to the deeps. Every now and again a lone individual could be seen busily trying to catch up with the others before disappearing into sapphire. The fact that a goddess was in their presence did not faze them in the slightest. Even the other people on the boat were not all that wary of her. Indeed, they might have given her a slightly wider berth than others but they were the type to do that with any outsider. *Such is the islander. Such is the solitude that can be found on the ocean.* Eris sat on her bench for hours, approached by no one and barely noticed as the pain in her chest steadily grew, the pressure weighing down her heart.

The velvet blanket of night fell upon the ferry. Stars twinkled above, having been given free reign by the Moon who had turned her face away. Leo and Hercules looked down, giving the story below a faint bit of interest. Other than her building sickness the day had been uneventful. Eris had not moved from her bench, the haver-sack making for a convenient pillow. The boredom had settled in rather quickly and counting the myriad uninhabited islands that drifted by had the same effect as counting sheep. When they passed Chios, she had been met with a soupy vision. *Ah yes, Chios. Now, that had been a good time. I could listen to that poet for hours. Well, I was involved in the War he sang of, but hey, it made for great poetry. So all is well. I wonder if it is still around – he had wondered if it would be.* She had fallen into a slumber at dusk, dreamless and light. Yet, now that the boat had fallen completely silent, something stirred her to waking.

She looked to the next bench and saw another figure, bent double and shaking. *What's going on here? Looks like another tale to become wrapped into.* She got up and walked carefully toward the figure. The person was covered in shadow but was obviously crying. They gripped a bundle tightly to their chest.

"*Kallinichta?*" Eris approached.

The person made to shrink back. "Leave me."

"I would, but it seems that you're upset over something."

They lifted their head. A young woman, no more than twenty, eyes large and dark. "Why do you care? Will you mock me too?"

Eris lifted a brow. "Why would I mock you?"

The woman offered her bundle. A baby's sleeping head poked from the top, resting though fitful. "His name is Maur."

Eris sat, staring at the baby. "And I should I mock you for this?"

"Because his...father...is not here. Not anywhere I know."

"I see. Nothing wrong with you two, though, as far as I see it."

"That is easy for you. You do not live like this."

"True. But I'm an outsider. I may as well not exist to most."

"Yet you could leave at any time. He is my anchor. He keeps me in this port. I do not hate my anchor. I keep the chain tight."

"But why are you crying?"

The mother sighed. "What life will Maur have? He has no father. People will look upon him as though he were an imp, a piece of trash. No amount of politics will alter his life – people are people. They will look down on him.

Nothing, they will think. He is nothing."

"Oh, I wouldn't say he was nothing", Eris replied. "He's here. And you love him, don't you?"

"Yes."

"Well, then, that's the most important part sorted. He'll be fine with you by his side. The fact that you're worried about him now is proof enough of that."

The woman's eyes settled on the baby. She stroked his head gently, so as not to wake him. "Is it? I should not have to worry. That is the fact of it. I am educated – I know that it would be the same no matter where I went. Except, perhaps, America. But how am I supposed to get there? I cannot. Our fate is in the hands of the Aegean. Why should I be looked at with mockery and scorn? What person has not dabbled in love before God intervenes? He went away before that could happen – my son is to be labelled illegitimate, a bastard. I only hope that he will be a better man than his father."

"With you I'm sure he will be."

"With luck and fate. Those are what govern the world."

Eris sighed. "Do you have anywhere to go?"

"No. I chose Rhodes to be as far away from gazes as possible. We shall farm goats and live without names. For all these people know his father is fighting the Bulgarians. That is what he shall be told. His father is a hero. My partner is a coward."

"I suppose that is best. Do you have anything?"

"No. I only know of an empty plot with an old shack on the island. He talked about it a couple of times. It is in the centre. I make my way there. It will be my farm."

Eris nodded. "Would you accept any help? From a stranger, I mean."

"Depends on what that help would be."

"Wait."

Eris returned with her haver-sack, digging into it. "Here", she said, "Where I'm going I won't be needing it."

The woman took the purse, peaking in. "No. That is too much."

"What do you mean?"

"There must be 500 drachma in there."

"Six, give or take. I want you to have it. As I say – I

won't be needing it."

"You are much too trusting. I could be a con-artist for all you know."

"That's as maybe. I doubt a con-artist would carry a baby around with them, though."

The woman smiled. "That is very true."

After a while, the woman got up and bid goodnight to Eris, leaving her on deck. *Mortals. A story for all, it seems. It's all just threads in the wind – some are caught and tangled, others simply float away. She'll be fine.* Not long after these thoughts Eris lay down to sleep again, trying to get comfortable on the wooden bench.

Her dreams were not going to be comfortable. Watch – the sea is throwing itself against the beach that borders the House of Discord. Eris is stood on the balcony perched on one of the highest roofs. It is built of marble, sat upon foundations of granite. The sea is a playful soul to begin with. But the storm-clouds build, the squall is promised. A cold breeze brushes her black hair across her cheek. Suddenly, lightening cracks the porcelain sky. It strikes the tiles of her roof, sending a great shudder through the structure. Now comes the noise. A great roar billowing from the horizon from the shadowy coastline of Rhodes. It shook the foundations, cracking them, making the pillars sway dangerously in the increasing wind. The goddess had no other recourse – she left the balcony just as it slipped from its moorings. With a crash it was followed by the pillars, one by one they fell in a danse macabre. Soon, all that was left was the roar, the wind, and lashings of rain that dampened her very bones. She was face down, only able to see one thing. A mosaic. The mosaic of the Apple. Kallisti was calling.

"I'm getting there!" She cried into the cacophony, "I'm so close!"

The tiles did not respond. The roar continued – an alarm going off, or a call for help. It got higher and higher in pitch: from roar, to screech, to whistle, finally staying at the cutting ring that had plagued her since Olympus. She screwed her eyes shut. There was a sensation of falling as she landed on the wood of the bench. Her eyes burst open, her arms flailed. The panic nearly set her sprawling on the deck. Seconds passed. Shaking calm took hold, bit by bit.

Soon the usual rhythm of her breathing returned, the cold sweat drying away. She took a deep breath. Dawn.

I must get to Rhodes.

Chapter Nine

The unsettled monotony of the Aegean was finally broken by the sight of Rhodes. With its coming came the promise of the journey's end – finally, the Apple was close. The ringing in Eris' ears did not cease, staying at a painful constant. As they approached she could not help but look around. *Oh. The Colossus has disappeared. Now, that is a shame. I wonder what happened there.* To her left walked the young woman from the night before. Eris beckoned to her.

"Do you see that?" She asked.

"Yes – Rhodes."

"Indeed. That's where your lives begin."

"How very idealistic."

"At least you found the strength to get here to begin with."

"…yes…Is there something you want?"

"Actually, I'm just wondering, what on Earth happened to the Colossus?"

The woman gave her a strange look. "An Earthquake.

In the 1300's."

"Hah, typical."

It took a much longer to dock than expected. As soon as the gangplank was dropped onto the quay the scene was akin to a jailbreak, the large crowd pushing their way off the boat as they rushed to the freedom of the land. Eris was the last to disembark, along with the young woman. They were not together long as the woman was swallowed by the crowd. *Well. I do hope that she finds all that she is looking for.* What mattered was that she was now on the island. All she had to do was find the man named Malcolm. *An Englishman. Shouldn't be too hard to find – the island is small enough for only one. They would most likely know him in the bars hereabouts. Now to pick one.*

She wandered into town, the houses clustering about each other in their need to get to the sea. The mid-morning was already warm, made hotter by the constant bustling. Indeed, for a while she was caught behind an eight-strong gang of fishermen carrying a full net to a stall, followed by a group of old women dressed completely in black.

Their faces were as dry and cracked as the road to Larissa. Rhodes was still a busy place, an island where lives could not help but noisily barge in on each other. Thankfully, it was still too early for a great many people to be attracted to the bars, leaving them relatively empty. Yet, wherever she asked, no one had even heard of this strange little Malcolm. She did not mention the Apple – word of that would surely spread quickly. It was just coming to the afternoon when she finally came to someone with information.

It was a small basement taverna, the type occupied by those who had careful, silent business to conduct. The barman turned slowly to meet her, not quite believing that she was stood there.

"Yes?" He coughed.

"Sorry, I'm looking for some information "

"P-police?"

"What? No. I'm looking for a man called Malcolm"

"Oh, yes, well. Can't be too careful nowadays. Rumblings are afoot. Malcolm, you say? Malcolm...English, is he?"

"Yes."

"I know him. Lives alone, old man. A shack on the coast – westward. About ten miles away. I've got to say, though, that the whole place feels just plain wrong. Can't explain it properly but it's got the same air as a graveyard. Utterly chilling. Still, ten miles oughtn't be that hard on the lady's feet should it?"

"I suppose not. Thank you."

"Not a problem, young lady."

As Eris left she could not but help feeling his gaze shifting over various places on her back. *Oh, how lovely.* Leaving the bar came with the feeling of a great release, her breathing becoming a little easier. *Right. At least I got some information. Let's just hope that it was true.* Just as she crossed the street she saw a group of five *gendarmerie* descend the stairs. *Well isn't that a good sign?* She hurried away before things turned for the rougher. Amongst the busyness of the place she was simply another person going about her day. Outsider she may have been, but a potential customer in equal measure. She crossed through the centre of the town, taking in the white buildings, hearing the church bells herald a new hour, pushing her way through the crowds that seemed to fill any available space. The bustle began to end when she finally met with the road out of town.

Memories of the happy farm workers of Álsostoukyparísi manifested as she walked down the dusty road. They had exhibited such a joy in living, in just being, without the need to think on what the next day may bring. That was something that had followed her through the journey – the need for motion, for movement. All through Greece were people living their lives, doing what they needed to do. Some were in a place they did not want, others in places unexpected, but is that not the very essence of chaos? *I believe it is. It does seem that my remit is somewhat more than random lightening hitting old donkeys or a mislaid rope causing a shipwreck. I'm more than the click of a finger.* Eris looked forward, knowing that her feet would not betray her, and allowed the sea breeze to cool her face as it set the fans of the windmills that stood like ragged hitch-hikers on the side of the road to spinning. There was something on that breeze, nearly a voice.

Kallisti. No wonder people think it feels wrong. A whispering on the wind, clawing at the ear. Almost makes me feel sorry for that idiot thief for having to live with it. The windmills creaked with their age in the light wind which brought the scent of citrus from inland. Yet the whispering was all that Eris could register. It was dragging her along, had dragged her all the way from Thessaly and beyond, bringing her closer to the source. *Perhaps that's why it took so long for me to notice that it had gone missing. It's quite hard to hear anything in the land of Mother Gaia – hard to do much at all. It had to cross worlds just to get to me. Oh, Kallisti, I'll be bringing you home soon.*

She was five miles out when she snapped. The strange quest and the people she had met had distracted her from the fundamental fact that she had been stolen from. Malcolm. The nasty little man who had made her suffer for the last few days. Malcolm. He who has done more damage than he will ever know. Malcolm. The interfering Englishman. She felt the rage building from her fingertips, making them tingle. Electric anger buzzed into her skull, sending pins and needles shooting down her spine. *How dare he?* The air around her cooled, beginning to lose its calm. The gentle breeze had dispersed – this was the telltale current of a storm on the way.

The landscape, beautiful in its desolation, seemed to close itself off. The sky was darkening. With every step the wind picked up. In the town, the old seamen hanging around the quay had worried looks on their brows. Never take the sea lightly, they said, for she can turn. The signs were there. One was nudged and off he went to clang on the storm bell. The town shuddered. Storms were the worst at this time of year. The people living near to the sea began to prepare for the crashing waves. Out on the Aegean, the ferry captain performed a small prayer – with God on side they might be able to dock at one of the smaller islets and find cover. On the island of Skiathos, a merchant and a writer were sharing a mint tea when the cold wind blew the latter's papers down the street.

"Do not worry about it, Yoni", the writer said, "Our lady is at work."

"If you say so, Alexandros. Things are afoot, methinks." The merchant grunted, shifting uneasily in his chair.

Even across the sea, beyond Volos, this discomfort was felt. A young woman, bent over a loom, shivered so violently that she dropped her needle.

"Will stop dropping that thing?" Her ancient aunt called.

"Sorry. Someone walked over my grave is all."

I hope she's alright.

The weight of these people, of these lives, bore upon Eris' shoulders. The whispers on the wind were now shouting wordless entreaties – they mingled with the infernal ringing in her ears in a Hellish choir. Kallisti was an either an object angry or an object excited. It called to her. *I'm being led. The damn thing has led me down a straight path – the most predictable path of all. Some things couldn't be foreseen but the rest of it, the linearity, that was a path well-trodden. Even this crescendo is simply the climax of the journey. It's needed. It'd be a flat journey without it. I'm not a dog on a leash!* And, with that, a wave came over her. Her eyes rolled back. She stumbled. Air was pushed from her lungs. *Alright. Fine. I'll keep going. I'm not happy. Not with you, not with foolish Malcolm.*

Rain began to patter into the dust, large globules that shattered against the stones and pummelled her hat. Faraway was a slight drum note of thunder. Electricity ran through the length of her arms and travelled along her shoulders. White hot, it bubbled away at her brain. What would she do to the man Malcolm once she got to him? As she climbed the crest of a slight hill she spotted a small, natural bay. In it stood an angular looking shack. *Found you.* She beelined toward it, making her own perilous path down to the sand. The smell of old fish permeated the air, not even dissipating in the heavy rain, finding its source in a pile of netting that settled beside the shack.

The one storey building looked to be built from any old piece of wood, a purely functional home that was set to collapse in the slightest breeze. This was a deception. In the growing wind there was an aura that was as warm and sickening as the heat from a dying man's brow. It radiated madness. The windows were small and dark, the door being anything other than rectangular. *He certainly profited from him little gain, didn't he?* She marched to the door and gave it three mighty knocks that had all the echo and cadence of funeral bells. Lightening flashed, giving the beach a garish shade. There was movement from within. Come on, little man, open the door. She knocked again. The knob turned slowly, the door crept open only a little.

"Who the bloody Hell are you?" Came an old voice.

"You ought to know. You stole from me."

"I have never stolen anything from any –"

Eris gave the door a mighty shove, tearing it from its hinges. "Look at me", she hissed. "Right at me."

The old man, sprawled on the floor, met her gaze. *She is going to kill me. Kill me for a mistake she's made.* He stared into those eyes and shuddered. Her anger glowed in the sockets, crimson in the storm shadow. They burned like dull coals. *Wait. Those eyes. It can't be. It can't be. Oh dear God.*

"E-Eris? Eris Discordia?"

"Correct, young Malcolm. Now, where is my Apple?"

"T-the Apple. Yes. I put it away. I'll go and get it."

He scrambled to a sloping chest of drawers on the other end of the room. Outside, the storm was reaching its apex. Wind clattered against the window panes of Rhodes. In the town, the shutters were closed against it, trying to fight the fingers prying them open. The roof titles shuddered as the onslaught slammed at them – the upper floors were all but abandoned, the attics utterly devoid of occupancy. The church was struck by a powerful lightning strike that shattered the rod, sending metal fragments spinning into the Cloisters below. The ferry had thankfully found a mooring at an unnamed islet and had been evacuated just before it was dashed heavily against the rocks, the passengers and crew watching it sink from the porch of a small cabin.

"Well", said the captain, whilst tuning his *oud*, "At least we're dry. And there's food."

Malcolm crawled to Eris, offering her a tightly wrapped bundle like a peasant offering their taxes to their lord. *That's it. The Apple.* She plucked it from his shaking hands and quickly stripped the rags away. It gleamed in the half-light and just about fit in the palm of one hand. *Kallisti. Oh, Kallisti. What've you been getting up to?* Her eyes moved from the Apple to the grovelling old man. *How truly pathetic.* The rage burst through her chest, a storm surge that none could stop. The shack shook with the constant buffeting of the wind, the walls creaking as they slowly began to come apart. She stepped forward, Kallisti weighing heavily in her hand.

"Wait."

"What?"

"I owe you an explanation."

"How about an apology? I'll be getting that in a few moments regardless. And I'll make damned sure that it is *sincere.*"

"I think that you should judge that for yourself."

"You shall speak. We have all the time we could possibly want."

Chapter Ten

The interior of the shack was austere – the necessary bed, chest of drawers, table, stove, boxes, and rickety stool was all that furnished the place. Light was provided by a single miner's lamp suspended from the ceiling which swayed with the movement of the roof. Eris chose to sit on the stool, allowing the portly Malcolm to take his place on the bed. The mattress, by the sound, was a spring affair that was threatening to turn on its owner at it earliest possible convenience. She stared blankly at him. Kallisti glowered in her lap like an overly loyal and protective cat. The wind kept its strength and the rain flowed through the ceiling and the door frame, drenching them both. The electricity that had been running through Eris' limbs and spine had increased, and was all but flickering from her fingertips. The ringing, however, had ceased. Peace was on the horizon.

"Well now, little thief, you've got my complete attention."

"C-can I start by saying that I am not a thief?"

"It's not the best start in my current mood."

"R-right. But it is nothing short of true. The thing is that, at the time, I was a travel writer. My publisher told me that he was sending people all over Europe and that I was the only person on the staff who could speak Greek. Well, I was here faster than the Spartans to Athens. The first stop was Cyprus and from there Thessaly, and then the Peloponnese. Not enough time for the islands, unfortunately. I got as far as Olympus. I climbed it, using an old path that seemed to have fallen out of use. Well, to cut a tawdry tale short, I accidentally found the Apple – "

"So, why did you steal it?"

"That is the thing – I did not steal it. It told me to take it."

"What?"

Malcolm gulped. "It told me to. I cannot explain it any better. I looked at it and I thought it absolutely beautiful. Certainly, the best craftsmanship I have ever seen and, to be honest, it looks just as it did then. Not a single blemish. But yes. It spoke to me. Now, I may speak the language but I was never a great student of the Classics. Even so, I know that to defy the will of the divine is not the best idea. Well, saying that, doing what they say often leads to a bad end but it is better to take the chance of being on the good side than the wrong – "

"How terribly misjudged."

"I – well. Indeed…still, that is why I took the Apple. From there it told me what to do. Get to Volos and go as far I could. So I walked for three days, never sleeping, to the port and came here. Though, I had to stay over at Skiathos for a couple of days. Half-mad I was. How that old priest thought it best to open his door to me I will never know. Still, here I came and took up residence in a boarding house, got a job on a trawler. Eventually, it told me to move again and I built this place."

"And that's it?"

"Yes. It told me to wait. I have not heard its ring for forty-five years. I'm glad that you've finally come, though. You're here to take it away."

Eris sat on her stool. The anger she felt still bubbled but its flow had changed, the direction heading away from the old man who faced her. It called attention to the Apple in her lap. *Kallisti. Guiding everything now, does it?*

"What now?" Malcolm's eyes were wide, his face paling.

Indeed. What now? There's no doubt that he's telling the truth. Too scared to lie. Damn it, Kallisti. Damn you for weaving a tale for me. Were you bored? Was that it? Needed to break your status quo with a little game? Well, congratulations, you've done it. And what a tale it is.

"The damage has been done", she said, "I'm going home."

With that, she stepped out of shack.

"Wait!"

"What?"

"Why aren't going to hurt me?"

"I suppose that is expected of me. That's why I'm not doing it"

She walked away from the door frame, leaving the old man stammering. *Time to go.* Outside, the wind had subsided, the rain falling softly and slowly turning into light drizzle. She clutched at Kallisti, its jet "K" contrasting sharply with the shine of the gold. Instead of the path leading to Rhodes, however, she turned on her heels and began her descent to the sea. The ringing immediately began anew. *No. I want to do this first. Then we go home.* The ringing subsided. Her feet crunched on the gravel path. It was well used, with a great amount of scrape marks adorning the stones.

The sea was bordered by a pebble beach that was just as utilitarian as the shack. A couple of yards leftward was a loosely built jetty constructed of wood and rope that made the sound of an old and neglected xylophone with every undulation of the waves. She stopped and crouched, dropping the haver-sack from her shoulder and proceeded to remove her hat and boots. Then she placed Kallisti in the bag. She stood and looked out to sea. The ringing came again.

"Not another word or I'll not come back for you again."

It fell silent. She walked forward, stopping at the tideline. The breeze was cold and salty, bringing moisture to her lips and her eyes. This was solitude. Not loneliness – the old adage that one can be completely alone in a room full of people is, indeed, true. Solitude is contemplative, a waking meditation which allows wordless thoughts to wander in and out of consciousness. Eris smiled.

She looked out to the horizon, allowing the water to caress her bare feet.

About The Author

Edwin Black would best describe himself as someone who looked like they have stepped out of the background of any given PG Wodehouse and dearly misses *le Belle Epoque*. He likes cats, books, and has a love of Greece. He currently resides in Sheffield.

He can be reached on Twitter at @EdwinBeatnik.

By the Same Author
The Edge of Everything

In the middle of the Yorkshire countryside sits a village like any other. It has a little shop, an out of order phone box, and a Victorian church.

It also has no children. And just down the road is a huge shadow which threatens to swallow it all.

Will anyone escape? Or will they fall from the Edge of Everything?

Available from Amazon and Airy Fairy, London Rd., Sheffield.

Lights Over Cithaeron: A Ghost Story

A lonely hiker makes his way along the slopes of Mount Cithaeron. Haunted by a bloody past he seeks only some peace. But there are forces on the mountain that ought not be disturbed, old places and ancient boundaries that should not be entered. Time waits in the shadows of Cithaeron, the echos of drums long past beat in its valleys. After a horrifying encounter there is no question of peace. There is only the need for survival.

And the lights over Cithaeron.

Available from Amazon.

Forthcoming

Music of the Spheres: Travels in the Land of Bek,

Life is not hard for Flynn and Jenk. The former works in the secretariat of a provincial bank, and the other is on the perpetual hunt for work. Over the course of one night, however, everything changes. The world comes to an end. Tasked with the impossible, the two last sane people in the world set off into the land of Bek on a journey that is darkness upon shadow...

The first of four parts.

Printed in Great Britain
by Amazon

54516519R00082